dearest love

BOOK TWO OF THE REBEL COURT

PREVIOUSLY ON

THE REBEL COURT
Catch Me

OTHER BOOKS BY ALIANNE DONNELLY

BLOOD AND SHADOWS
Blood Moons
Blood Trails
Blood Debts
Blood Hunt

DAWN OF RAGNAROK
The Royal Wizard
Dragonblood
Prince of Deceit

THE BEAST
Bastien
The Beast

OTHER TITLES
Wolfen
Virtual
Function: L1VE

dearest love

ALIANNE DONNELLY

Rebel heroes deserve rebel dedications. With that in mind...

I am dedicating this story with love to the naked Viking at the Renaissance Faire. Your furry loincloth and horned helmet grace the makeshift streets of a faux-Elizabethan England every year, rain or shine. And that kind of willfully anachronistic defiance deserves praise. Well done, good sir. Skål!

CHAPTER 1

Ten years ago, somewhere in the Elderwood…

Just a few more minutes… Dammit! Another candle burned down, turning the cavern pitch-black. And they didn't have any more.

Beau breathed in deeply to stave off panic. Their main supply lines had been severed, but the Rebels had others; they just took a little longer to deliver, that was all. Another shipment would be delivered any day now, he was sure of it.

Careful not to disturb the map he'd been drawing on, Beau stood, rounded the desk, and shuffled out into the main tunnel.

Blessed light. This cave system used to be a diamond mine. Now it served as the Rebels' stronghold and base of operations, and the nineteen-year-old Beau, as their master strategist, had been tucked all the way in the farthest reach of the most convoluted tunnel for safe keeping. After Snow White herself, Beau was the most important person in this war.

He emerged into the main cave—a massive, natural cathedral currently housing the bulk of their meager supplies and a handful of foot soldiers passing through to give their progress reports to Snow. Here, several small campfires and three great fairy light orbs banished the shadows, but what they illuminated was almost worse than the darkness: gaunt bodies, harried faces, haunted eyes.

Beau walked among them, taking note of every shaking hand and every unshed tear. Darius and Sebastian were sitting together near the back, resting after a successful defense campaign. Graeme, standing guard at the mouth of the cave, wore a slightly darker scowl than usual. With Saxon down for the count and Haig gone, Graeme had first, second, and third watch until someone else could relieve him—

"Boo!"

Startled, Beau looked down at the girl who'd just snuck up on him. Her big, blue eyes gleamed bright in her sooty face as she grinned at him as if she'd just won a game of hide-and-seek. "What are you doing here?" he demanded, doing his best to look tall and intimidating.

The infuriating brat giggled. "What are *you* doing here? I thought you weren't allowed to come out of your cave."

Beau scowled. "That's what you get for eavesdropping. Half the story and no context to understand what you're talking about. Go away, Lily. I don't have time for you right now."

Lily's smile dropped. "I'm sorry." Then she turned on her heels to shuffle away, dragging her feet to add to his guilt.

He sighed. "Wait."

Lily stopped, turned back around, but didn't raise her head. Her flaming red curls, even tousled and tangled, shone like copper around her. At fourteen, she already had the makings of an unparalleled beauty, and Beau pitied every man who took a fancy to her. Lily would play them like a fiddle and send them packing after she was done.

"Why *are* you out here?" he asked. "Is something wrong?" Miss Kiki and her girls were rescues from a fire Zorana's troops had set to the brothels in Kesteran. They'd lost their home and place of business, but had escaped with their lives and dignities, which was more than others had. Yet even with Snow White assuring the women they were safe here, Miss Kiki didn't want any of her girls around the men, especially her too-young niece, Lily.

Lily hitched her bony shoulders up to her ears. "No one wants to talk to me in there. They think I'm too young for them to tell me what's going on, but I still hear them whispering about it. I thought… Well, I hoped…" Pushing her hair out of her face, she gazed up at him. "You're the closest to my age here. I know you're super busy and all but…" She stared helplessly, at a loss for words. Then, seeming to light on an idea, she fumbled in her pockets and pulled out a pair of wooden dice so old their dots were almost completely rubbed off. "I have these! Will you play with me? Please?"

Beau looked from the sorry state of those dice—probably shaved to rig the game—to her pathetically hopeful expression. Without more candles, he couldn't do any proper work, anyway. What harm could it do to play dice for a little while? "I suppose I can spare a few minutes."

The radiant smile Lily gave him all but broke his heart. She grabbed his hand and tugged him to a secluded outcropping with a patch of smooth floor to play on. After yanking him down to sit beside her, she placed the dice in his hand. "You go first."

"You'll lose," he warned. "Are you ready for that?"

She scoffed. "Sweetheart, I was born ready."

He laughed and threw the dice.

They played until his ass hurt and his legs went numb. For hours, the two of them bounced a pair of decidedly shady dice against the cave wall, making outrageous wagers neither of them could ever cover: money, jewels, lumber, raw magic wells. And for those few hours, Beau felt neither poor, nor scared, nor tired.

"Your turn," he said, his face hurting from grinning more than he had in the last year and a half. "Three Clydesdales and a milking goat says you can't roll a seven."

Lily rattled the dice in her hand, considering the wall with the intensity of someone staring down an opponent on a dueling field.

"Well? Do you take the bet?"

"I don't have horses, or goats."

He shrugged. "Bet something else, then."

With a quicksilver glance sideways, she threw the dice, declaring, "I'll wager a kiss."

Beau had barely registered the words before the dice settled. A two and a six. She'd lost.

They stared in silence at the faded black dots as the cave got dimmer, hotter. And the silence stretched on, getting more awkward by the second. *Say something!* he thought as he slowly collected the dice. *Say it's getting late and you have work to do. Laugh it off and say you'll collect that kiss when she grows up. No, too dangerous. Say—*

Lily's cool hand touched his cheek, turned his face toward her, and then she pressed her lips to his. Beau sat frozen, hands curled into fists on the cold cave floor while his face burned. He wasn't breathing. Should he be breathing? Should he kiss her back? She was just a kid, for crying out loud!

Lily spared him additional embarrassment when she let go of him and drew back. Gods, he almost followed. What was wrong with him? She searched his gaze, then blushed and gave him a shy little smile so unlike her exuberant grins it felt like a punch in the gut. "Thanks for playing with me," she said, then pushed to her feet and ran off, leaving the dice behind.

He was still staring into the dark tunnel where she'd disappeared when Graeme shouted for help from the cave entrance. Swiftly pocketing the dice, he hobbled over to see what happened.

Graeme half-dragged, half-carried a bloodied Haig through the cave, yelling at the crowd to part. *Holy gods…*

"Make way! *Move!*" Beau hurried ahead, pushing people aside to clear the tunnel to Declan's infirmary. He spared Snow a grave look, but she couldn't leave the troops in the middle of their reports, not even for one of her Rebel Seven.

Once they made it to the infirmary, Graeme helped Haig onto a cot, careful of the bleeding cuts all over his back. "What the hell happened to you, man?" he growled.

"Ambush," Haig said, wincing as Declan rolled him to lie on his front and tore off the bloodied shirt to reveal long gashes so deep Beau could see glimpses of bones.

His stomach dropped, knees weakening. "What ambush? Where were you?" He hadn't ordered any actions in days; they'd lost too many men in the last one and he'd needed time to strategize their next attack.

Haig turned his head to look at him. "Don' worry 'bout it," he said, then moaned in pain when Declan began to wipe away blood from the few patches of unharmed skin he still had. "My fault. Got cocky. But it's done. Mission accomplished, like I promised." He was shaking, his teeth chattering.

Then his words registered, and Beau shared a confused look with Declan. "What mission?" Beau asked. Had he missed something?

Haig tried to roll his shoulder and ended up hissing in pain and biting down so hard on his own arm he drew blood.

In an instant, Declan went into full-on healer mode. "Everyone out. I need room to work."

Graeme dragged Beau out of the infirmary by his sleeve. "Think long and hard," he snarled. "What did you do? Where did you send him?"

"I…didn't," Beau replied numbly.

"He said something about the supply lines when he showed up."

Beau shook his head. Trying to figure out what possible reason he might have had to send Haig out alone, all he could think of were maps. Supply lines severed, one after the other. Strategic hits that must have been planned out with meticulous care, well ahead of time.

Had he suspected another mastermind in Zorana's forces?

He couldn't remember!

Graeme's ominous scowl cleared slightly as he sighed. "Look, I know you didn't do it on purpose. We've been putting a lot on your shoulders—we're all counting on you to think us out of this mess, and it isn't fair. You're just a kid, for fuck's sake. You should be chasing pretty girls and playing dice, not wasting away in a fucking burrow. So I get it, okay? We all slip. We all make mistakes. But we can't afford them from you. If you fuck up, we all die. Understand?"

Beau nodded, staring at the far wall, only half-hearing the words as he kept slamming against the same dead end in his own reasoning: Why would he have ordered Haig out on assignment? *Why?*

"Graeme," Declan said from the doorway. "Haig wants to talk to Beau."

"He should be out cold by now," Graeme snapped. "Didn't you sedate him?"

"I tried," the Ravenskin healer replied evenly. "He insists on speaking to Beau first."

All three of them returned to Haig's bedside. Haig's eyes were half closed and unfocused, his hands loose over his head. Declan had covered his back with a light sheet of bandage that was already soaked red with blood. Looking at him, Beau was terrified Haig wouldn't make it through the night.

After an encouraging nod from Declan, Beau sank to his haunches to put himself in Haig's line of vision. "Hey, man," he said as calmly as he could.

Haig blinked. "Hey, kid. How're ya doin'?"

"Better than you. What happened?"

Haig winced, sucking in a pained breath. "Bastard had assassins guarding him. Six of 'em. Shoulda seen that coming."

"Who are you talking about?"

"Shoulda retreated when they came out. Had a way out, but… woulda lost…surprise. Had to get it done. No matter the cost."

The words chilled Beau to the bone. "If the cost is your life, it fucking matters!"

Haig choked out a chuckle. "That's cute, kid, really. Listen. 'm 'bout to pass out here in a second but…tell the Network: Strike now. Strike hard. Get out…quick…" His eyes closed and his mouth went slack.

"It's okay," Declan assured them. "He's just sleeping. He'll be fine once I close the wounds, but he'll hurt like hell for a while. We're down one man for the time being."

Beau pushed to his feet to find Graeme frowning at him. "Didn't you say last week you were waiting for an opportunity to strike at Zorana's spies?"

Beau nodded. "I seem to recall I had a plan in mind, but I can't remember what it was."

Graeme uttered a long string of foul curses. "I know what this is," he said, rubbing a hand over his face. "Get the word out to your Network as fast as you can, got it? And after that, I want you to take a few days' break."

"But—"

"We can handle things without you for a little while. You planned well ahead for any contingency—"

"Yet I somehow missed *this*?" Gods, how could he have missed this?

"Trust me, kid, you didn't. Go. Do what you need to do. I'll tell the others."

Later, once his mind had cleared, Beau would remember this conversation and get furious that the others had left him in the dark about something that could have cost Haig his life. For now, he was too rattled to do anything except mumble a message to his runner and then walk aimlessly through the cave system.

Somehow, he ended up sitting on the ground just off the main tunnel, far enough to hide in shadow, but close enough to see the light.

And somehow, when he woke up a while later, he found himself clutching an old pair of dice so hard they'd left sharp impressions in the palm of his hand.

CHAPTER 2

Present Day, Miss Kiki's House of Pleasure…

Lily Maverick was just returning to her apartments after a successful kitchen raid when someone grabbed her by the arm and yanked her into the employee hallway. Busted! But before she could break free and protest her innocence, a wad of cash appeared in front of her nose and a familiar voice said, "I want to hire you."

Wait. She knew that voice. But no, that didn't make any sense…

Her captor released her arm and brought forth another wad of cash, completely blocking him from view. "F-for a week," he stuttered. "To start."

This must be what a stroke feels like. Lily moved the money away from her line of sight. Behind it was none other than Beau Legeare, one of the legendary Rebel Court, who hung out with his friends in a brothel, but ran for the door whenever a girl—namely Lily—tried to sit on his lap.

That Beau Legeare wanted to hire her?

What had Cooke put into those damn chocolate meringues?

"Well? Say something," he demanded, his handsome face flushed beet red. He wore his formal uniform: white trousers, white shirt, and a sleeveless white leather jerkin with the hood lying flat against his back. Designed by Snow White herself, the uniform was a mark of honor for her long-time allies and friends. Unmistakable, irreplicable, and shut-up-and-fuck-me hot.

Lily was seconds away from doing something incredibly stupid, like swooning. "Say again?"

If possible, Beau flushed a deeper red, and a faint sheen of sweat broke out over his forehead. He stuffed the money and his hands into his pockets and rocked back on his heels. "I want to hire you for a week. I want twenty-four-hour access, starting immediately. Money's no object. I can promise you nothing weird, and you can still keep your other appointments during that time, but I will require use of your apartment here. Name your price."

Be still my beating heart... That sounded so rehearsed, Lily almost got offended. This was either a dare of some kind or, given his uniform, something to do with crown business. Since Beau always went out of his way to avoid her, the latter was most likely, but then why not just say so? Lily wasn't an idiot, and all of the Rebels knew Miss Kiki and her girls were loyal to the death. "Why me?" Would he tell her the truth?

His eyes widened like a frightened deer. "W-we have history," he said after a panicked pause.

Aaaand that's a no *on the truth.* "Why now?" *One more chance.*

Beau backed up a step, but she followed, closing the distance between them once more. "Why not now?" he countered. If Lily didn't know for a fact that Beau was one of the smartest men in Valefort...

"Because in the ten years you've known me, you've barely acknowledged my existence. And now suddenly you're all eager to get into bed with me. Literally." *Not impressing me with those legendary smarts, sport.* The physique, on the other hand... *Whew!*

Beau's shoulders drew back, he rooted his feet, and raised his chin like a warrior about to endure untold tortures, but his eyes betrayed him. Uncertainty flickered in their jewel green depths, making them seem darker, almost like evergreens.

When he opened his mouth to deliver whatever spiel he'd rehearsed, she cut him off. "Is it because you're finally ready to give up your V-card?"

The way his jaw went slack would have been hilarious, if not for the fact Lily had only wanted to tease him. Oh, she knew he was shy with women and didn't get out much, but he was almost thirty, for crying out loud! *Someone* should have locked that up long ago. *Holy gods, he really is a virgin!*

Beau pulled himself together again, took one more step away from her, and hit the wall at his back. Lily followed without hesitation, trailing a fingertip down the center of his chest. "Couldn't find any-one to *relieve* you of it?" That had come out more breathy than she'd intended.

Couldn't be helped. In the face of this life-changing revelation, even his ulterior motives didn't matter anymore. The idea of Beau Legeare, completely innocent, untouched, and in her grasp did wick-ed things with her insides. She felt butterflies in her belly and heat gathering between her legs. After a lifetime spent walking on spiked stilettos of ridiculous heights, her ankles became unsteady and Lily leaned forward, as much for balance as to get closer. She ached to feel his arms around her, even if it was just to steady her—and he did pull his hands out of his pockets as if to do exactly that, but he stopped just short of touching her.

His clothes were imbued with the scent of ink and old books, but underneath that, his essence was all man: earthy, warm, mouthwa-tering. She wanted to curl up and rub herself all over him to get that scent on her skin. A deeply physical creature, Lily enjoyed every as-pect of intimacy in all of its forms.

But Beau didn't. He avoided touching beyond a brief hearty hand-shake—Lily'd seen him wince and go rigid when one of his comrades put his arm around Beau's shoulders, and even a peck on the cheek made him blush.

And now he wanted to hire her.

Ten years she'd been nursing her crush on the legendary Beau Legeare, the unsung hero of Snow White's war against the evil queen. Ten years she'd watched him stroll in and out of Miss Kiki's, make pleasant conversation with the girls, and never touch a single one. Ten years she'd dreamed of what it'd be like to have him look at her and truly *see* her. Did he now, finally?

"If you feel weird about paying me, don't," she told him, then raised up on tiptoe to whisper at his ear, "The first one is always on the house."

"Stop," he gasped, pushing her away just enough to slip free and put some distance between them. Breathing hard, he paced a few steps deeper into the hallway, then back again, raking his light brown hair into glorious disarray. He looked half-crazed and she'd barely touched him. "This has to be on my terms."

Play it cool. Don't scare him off. She leaned back in the same spot where he'd stood, propped her heel against the wall, and drew her shoulders back, pushing her breasts forward. Beau's gaze snared on her corseted cleavage in an instant. *Yes, want me,* she silently willed. *Want me as much as I want you.* "Of course," she replied. "Name your terms."

It took him a second to tear his gaze away from her breasts. When he did, he seemed at a loss.

"You'll want to set the pace, naturally," she offered.

"Right," he said, then cleared his throat. "Yes. Absolutely."

"And you'll probably want control over everything. Setting, position, things like that."

Beau nodded. "Yes. All of it."

"And we'll be wanting to keep this…secret?"

A quicksilver frown twitched across his brow. "Secret?"

"I mean, you obviously ambushed me back here for a reason, right?" *Pause and watch him start to panic.* "You don't want your friends to know you're still…you know."

He straightened with what almost looked like relief. "Right. Yes, of course. No, I don't want anyone to know that. That'd be embarrassing."

Regardless of his reasons, Beau had still come to her over all of the other girls. That had to mean something. Lily grasped onto that notion, even knowing it was only a pretty lie. But oh, how pretty it was…

"So? Do you accept?" And there he went, pulling out those wads of money again. "How much?"

Dammit! You were doing so well! "Big spender, booking a whole week for your first time. You sure you can keep it up that long?"

Beau ducked his chin, dropping his gaze to the floor. "I guess we'll see."

She'd embarrassed him. Well, good. He deserved it for waving money in her face like she was some cheap whore. Lily might be a whore, but she was in no way cheap! And besides, they did have history. The pathetic thing was, if he'd come to her with nothing but the truth on his lips, she would have welcomed him with open arms and never asked for a thing. She would have taken whatever he'd chosen to give her and then let him walk out of her life again, blissfully happy with that little scrap for the rest of her life.

But he'd started out with a *lie*. Which meant Lily would never be satisfied with anything less than everything now. And, by the gods, she would get it.

His V-card was no longer enough. For insulting her intelligence, impugning her honor, and toying with her feelings—wittingly or not—Lily would demand a much higher price.

She would make her rebel fall head over heels.

Lily adjusted her corset, then sashayed toward him and, for the second time in fifteen minutes, pushed perfectly good money away. "Tell you what. Why don't you let me keep a running tally? When we're finished, I'll give you a bill and you can settle up before you leave. Sound good?"

His Adam's apple moved up and down in a loud *gulp*. "Do you want me to sign anything to make it official?"

How sweet. "We don't like paperwork around here. Our deals are sealed with a kiss."

Beau stared into her eyes for a delicious, uncertain moment. When he moved, it was slow, unsure. His gaze dropped to her lips, then his hand came up to her face. His cool fingers skimmed her skin, but she felt goose bumps from just that small contact and barely suppressed a shiver. Then, finally—*finally*—he pressed his mouth to hers.

A couple of seconds of pressure, then Beau wavered, as if he would withdraw again, and Lily held still, waiting for him to decide. To her delight, he stayed. His lips briefly brushed over hers, a sweet echo of their kiss ten years ago, and an aching tightness lodged in her throat. She'd never forgotten that night, the innocence of playing dice, and the rush of stealing a small taste of what she'd imagined to be a fated love. She leaned closer to kiss him back, softened and opened just the slightest bit—an invitation, nothing more. His breath puffed against her cheek as he shifted his feet closer. His hands came up to rest on her hips, then snaked around her waist, pulling her fully into his embrace.

Lily felt him tremble the slightest bit and wanted to somehow communicate that he had no reason to ever be nervous with her. There was nothing in the world she'd rather be doing; no place she'd rather be than right here in his arms.

She took his bottom lip between hers, sucked on it just enough to make his breath catch, flicked her tongue over it while her hands came to rest on his shoulders. Beau deepened the kiss slowly, licking into her mouth at first, only to trace the cutting edge of her teeth as if testing the waters. But when Lily dared to meet him, everything changed. His breath hissed in a startled gasp, and he tensed for a moment, his heart thumping so hard, Lily felt it against her breast. She was half afraid he would pull away again and prepared herself for the setback, when he suddenly tightened his hold on her so hard her feet came up off the floor. With one arm around her waist, he speared his free hand into her hair to hold her still as he walked her back until she felt the wall against her shoulder blades.

And then the timid, shy, virginal Beau Legeare snapped his leash. He devoured her mouth with plunging strokes, his tongue sparring with hers over and over as their lips mashed together so hard it almost hurt. His fingers dug hard into her hip and scalp; his knee pressed between her legs, leaving her breathless, dizzy with delight and hope.

Lily hooked her leg over his hips to keep him close, clutched at his nape, and kissed him back, seeking out every secret and every flavor, committing every detail to memory. If their first kiss had warmed her dreams, their second scorched her soul. And she never wanted it to end.

All at once, he pulled away with a hissed curse. Her mind disoriented and pleasure-hazed, Lily barely registered when he pulled her into the shadows of an unlit alcove and pressed his hand over her mouth. Only then did she come to her senses enough to hear voices coming down the hallway: two girls just off an appointment, joking and comparing notes for the lover they'd just shared. Their high-pitched laughter bounced off the velvet-covered walls and stabbed into her ears.

When they were gone, Beau finally remembered himself and re-leased her, stepping back as far as the alcove would allow. "I'm sorry," he said. "Did I hurt you?"

Physically? "No."

"I didn't mean to be so rough. It's just…really important that no one knows I'm here."

"Are you that ashamed of being a virgin?"

She couldn't see him flush in the dim light, but she did hear his breathing change.

"Or is it me you're ashamed of? Being here, paying for my company."

He didn't answer.

Might as well have stabbed her through the heart. "I see."

"Lily—"

"Hey, no big. I'm providing a service. You're paying for it. It's just a business transaction, nothing more. And like you said, you set the terms. If you want privacy, you got it. Come on." Lily took his hand and pulled him across the hall to a sconce that opened a secret stair-well. The brothel was riddled with passageways like this, remnants of a war that had almost destroyed all of Valefort. Hardly anyone used them anymore, but this particular one happened to be a handy shortcut to her apartment on the second floor.

As they felt their way through the darkness, Lily counted her steps, her mind turning over what might have been the greatest dilemma of her life: how to make Beau Legeare fall in love and not break her own heart.

CHAPTER 3

Y ou're right, Beau. *The traitor has to be one of my nobles. I need you to find out who it is.*"

Three sentences, and Beau was up the creek.

In some distant corner of his mind that wasn't reeling from the enormity of his situation, he knew it made sense. Valefort had a traitor. A member of Snow White's board of directors was engaged in insider trading—an offense punishable by death according to the word of the Charter. Someone like that could not be accused without irrefutable evidence of wrongdoing, and the queen had charged Beau with acquiring said evidence.

Except the information they had gathered so far pointed to messages being passed back and forth inside Miss Kiki's brothel and the acquiring of said evidence involved Beau staking out the place to learn the traitors' identities. Gods, the irony… Of all the Rebel Court, Beau was inarguably the *least* qualified to spend any length of time inside any brothel, let alone this one.

Case in point: here he was, two minutes after securing himself unhindered access to the facility, being dragged up a pitch-black, hidden stairwell by Lily Maverick, who thought he'd hired her to "give up his V-card."

How did she even know he'd never…that he…

Just when his senses began to adjust to the darkness, Lily threw open another door and stepped straight into a blinding shaft of sunlight, throwing him all over again when she pulled him inside and slammed that door shut.

"Make yourself comfortable," she said, and Beau froze.

He'd expected red velvet, satin sheets, and hosiery strewn all over the place. But this? Cozy, worn furniture, big windows, painted wooden rafters… This neat, adorable little private nook was completely out of place in a brothel. Lily had obviously taken great pains to turn it into a home, and the starving street urchin in him didn't know how to process that.

Make myself comfortable?

"I don't usually bring clients up here," she said, and for the first time he detected a hint of uncertainty in her voice.

"Do you want to go somewhere else?" It didn't matter to Beau where he set up camp, as long as it gave him privacy and access to the common room.

She shrugged. "You wanted twenty-four-seven access to my apartment. What the customer wants, the customer gets."

Beau winced at her curt tone. "Listen, about before, I didn't mean to be so abrupt with you." Not his finest moment, but hell, he was lucky he'd managed to speak full sentences. Beau had ten years of pent-up longing for this woman bottled up so tight inside, most of the time he forgot it existed. But whenever Lily appeared, it all came roaring to the surface and completely scrambled his brains.

"It's all right," she replied gamely. "Believe it or not, I've had worse."

When she reached for the fastenings on his jerkin, he flinched away. "Wait! Just… Give me a second here." *Barely keeping it together.*

Seeming to understand, she nodded. "Take all the time you need." But then she pulled the top curves of her corset together and started unhooking it, one loop at a time.

"W-what are you doing?"

Her eyes sparkled with mischief as she grinned, showing off a pair of dimples. "Getting naked." Two more hooks slid free, and now he could see the inner curves of her breasts where they pushed together.

"Thought you'd like to see the goods before you sample."

He wasn't breathing. Should he be breathing?

Two more hooks, down to her belly button now, and the wicked little ring pierced through it. Beau almost whimpered. His palms grew embarrassingly moist, and he was starting to sweat underneath his uniform.

"So where would you like to do this?" she asked, and it took him a moment to tear his gaze away from the corset dropping to the floor to look at her face. He stared hard, willing himself not to glance lower, but even without focusing there, he still saw the blurry shape of her naked torso, her gorgeous breasts displayed without a hint of shyness. Lily was soft and curvy in all the right places, with generous hips and a plump belly that was usually disguised with a corset. He much preferred her without it.

"Beau?"

He blinked to moisten his eyeballs, still staring at her face. "Yes?"

"Do you want to go to the bedroom?"

"Uhh…" *Calm down. Calm the fuck down!*

"Or stay here, on the couch?"

"Well—"

"Or, if you want to be really adventurous…" She walked past him, then swung open a bookcase he hadn't even noticed before and stepped out onto a balcony. Hoots and whistles echoed from down below when she spun around and leaned against the railing. "What do you say, handsome? Do you feel like taking a walk on the wild side?"

Beau somehow forced his feet to move a step closer and gaped. The balcony overlooked the brothel's common room. Its floor was all glass, giving everyone below an unobstructed view of her, and the railing was constructed from wrought iron bars, one of which was currently riding the valley between her buttocks, if the cheers from below were any indication.

Lily smiled over her shoulder, bent her knees to slowly sink a few inches lower, then pushed upright again and wriggled her fingers at them before pushing off and sashaying back into the apartment. "No, you're right. You're not ready for that yet." She guided the bookcase back into place and latched it securely closed. "Listen, I know you're nervous, okay? So tell me what would make you feel more at ease."

"Being invisible," he replied without thinking.

To his surprise, Lily smiled brightly. "Well, darling, why didn't you just say so?" She touched his arm as she passed by him to a wooden chest tucked in the corner. After rifling through things that made all sorts of interesting sounds, she pulled out a necklace. "There!" She turned back, but stopped a couple of steps away. "Are you going to freak out again if I touch you?"

If the earth swallowed me whole right now, would anyone really miss me? "I'll try not to."

She approached him as she would a wild animal, slowly, without making any sudden moves, and he bent over so she could loop the necklace around his neck, the motion bringing his nose almost to her shoulder. He caught a hint of her perfume, but it was the clean scent of woman underneath it that had his eyelids lowering to half-mast and his body swaying forward. He felt the heat of her skin and wanted nothing more than to bring it against him, bask in it for the rest of time.

Then she stepped back with a satisfied smile. "I completely forgot I still had that. All the girls got one back in the day. For clients who want to stay anonymous."

"You mean you can't see me now?" He didn't feel any different. And he could still see himself.

Lily shrugged. "Go check it out. Bathroom has a huge mirror."

He followed her pointing finger through the connecting bedroom door to the one leading to the bathroom. Like the rest of the apartment, it was cozy and clean, and in the mirror above the sink, Beau saw nothing but a slight disturbance in the air. Of course, that still didn't mean anything. So he went back to the bookcase and stepped out onto the balcony.

The people below cheered again, but the whoops quickly turned into disappointed hums. He looked at each face carefully, saw gazes shift left and right, clearly looking for someone who wasn't to be seen. *It works!* Mind whirring a million miles an hour, Beau realized Lily had just given him the best tool for accomplishing his mission.

Not just the ability to observe without being seen, but also a place to do it from where he had an unobstructed view of practically the entire establishment.

He came back in, all set to thank her, but stopped dead in his tracks at the sight of her with her back to him, bent at the waist, rolling one thigh-high down her shapely leg. Beau locked his knees to keep from falling over. *Holy gods!*

Beau cleared his throat to let her know he was back in the room.

Still bent over, she smiled in his general direction and went to work on baring the other leg. "So I just got a brilliant idea."

Uh-oh.

"How about we get to know each other a little? Physically, I mean. Now, don't panic. You don't need to do anything." The insubstantial piece of rolled-up fabric pooled around her foot, and she slowly straightened, grinning over her shoulder. "Unless you want to." Hooking her fingers into the waist of her panties, she tugged them down over her hips, then let them fall to the ground and gingerly stepped out of them.

Totally naked, except for those ridiculously high heels and the thigh-highs adorning her ankles like the most decadent jewelry, she pivoted to face him and said, "I'll start."

Beau couldn't tear his gaze away. She was perfection covered in soft, creamy skin and nothing else. Her groin was completely smooth, and Beau'd never thought he'd be one of those guys, but the sight of it completely shut down his higher intellect.

"As you can see, I'm not shy. I'm not ashamed of what I do. I love sex, and touch, and intimacy. I love how my body feels when it moves, when it's teased and filled—gods, especially that last." Her hands ran down her sides, over her belly. She brushed her own nipples back and forth, mesmerizing him with the hypnotic rhythm before she slipped one hand between her legs and stroked herself. "And I love being watched. It turns me on something crazy." With a moan, she brought her hand out to show him moisture glistening on her fingers. "Do you want to watch me make myself come?"

He'd never gone so hard so fast before in his life. Zero to near-spontaneous-orgasm in two seconds flat, and it was all he could do not to come in his pants then and there.

Without waiting for his answer, Lily turned on her heels and walked into the bedroom, and Beau was helpless not to follow the sway of her hips, mesmerized by the dimples over her ass.

His shin slammed into the edge of her coffee table. Beau cursed up a blue streak, but at least it cooled his heels a little bit. That is, until she turned her head sideways and smiled. She'd heard.

In over my head…

She climbed onto the bed on all fours, and Beau's feet stuck in the doorway. With her back to him, she went down on one elbow and arched her back, displaying her sex in all its glistening glory.

…and sinking ever deeper…

When Lily reached down and spread herself, Beau had to grab onto the doorjamb to stay on his feet. Dripping wet already, she spread the moisture all over the lips of her sex and her clit and crooned, "Feel free to jump in any time."

I'll never surface again.

Beau couldn't take a full breath. His cock throbbed in his pants, seconds away from going off, and he hadn't even touched Lily yet.

She spread her knees wider, arched her back further, leaned her shoulders to the mattress, and began stroking herself with both hands, showing him without words exactly how she liked to be touched. She rubbed her clit, massaged her lips, undulating her hips in wanton invitation. He couldn't even call it a tease anymore; Lily was so lost in her own pleasure, she barely spared him a look. Her hand drenched, she slipped two fingers into her pussy, slow and deep. She pulled them out again, rubbed a tight circle around her clit, then plunged back in.

She squirmed, panted, moaned her pleasure, while Beau stood there, thoroughly entranced, imagining they were his hands on her; his cock. That thought pulled a shudder out of him, and he reached for his zipper, unable to resist anymore.

As if she'd heard, Lily licked her lips, twisted a little to look his way out of the corner of her eye, then went right back to fucking herself with her fingers, and Beau's hand matched the heady rhythm of hers, pumping up and down in time with her thrusts. Picking up speed, she slid her fingers in and out, harder, faster, whimpering, undulating her hips as if she couldn't hold still any longer.

At last, when Beau's panting grew as loud as hers, she let herself go, crying out. And she kept stroking, purring her pleasure until Beau couldn't take it anymore. But he stayed rooted in place, cock in hand, waiting with bated breath to see what she'd do next.

Lily pushed off the bed and sauntered over to him. She came close enough for him to catch a hint of her intimate scent, and he squeezed the base of his cock hard.

Then she raised the hand she'd fucked herself with. "Care for a taste?"

Shocked to his core, Beau leaned forward and took her fingers in his mouth, licking her salt straight from her skin, sucking it clean. He drank in her reaction, the way her lips parted on a delicate sigh, and her eyelids lowered to half-mast. She rocked up on her toes toward him, her other hand blindly fumbling along his invisible torso to place him in the doorway.

When that hand strayed too far south for his comfort, he released her fingers, picked her up by the waist, and tossed her back onto the bed, following right behind.

Beau kissed the surprised squeal from her lips, pinned her down with his weight. *Don't change your mind,* he prayed. *Don't ask me to stop.* He honestly didn't think he could.

The head of his cock slid between the lips of her sex, closer to paradise than he'd ever dreamed of getting. Lily reached down, guided him into place, hiccuped a gasp as he rammed home so deep, he slammed up against her clit in the process. *Hot... So hot.* Her body squeezed him, pulling him deeper.

He lasted two more thrusts, before the pleasure overwhelmed him and he came so hard, his eyes almost rolled back in his head.

CHAPTER 4

Beau's ears rang and his vision hazed over, and for a moment he was deaf and blind to everything but the most intense pleasure he'd ever felt in his life. It was so far beyond anything he'd ever felt on his own, his brain couldn't process it at first. When it did, he remembered he wasn't alone, and looked down at the woman he'd wanted so badly for a full third of his entire life, an apology on the tip of his tongue.

Instead, he watched her gorgeously red lips part, felt her hand working between them as she stroked herself to the orgasm he hadn't lasted long enough to give her. Lily arched into him, her breasts pressing into his chest, and he felt her inner muscles squeeze around his cock still inside her. Beau bit back a groan, too embarrassed to enjoy the sensation.

Not knowing what else to do, he palmed her breast, rubbing his thumb over her puckered nipple. To his surprise, she moaned and her pussy clenched down hard on him, making his cock twitch in response. Breath left him. Gods, she was so beautiful, it hurt.

Heat flooded his cheeks, and he pulled away, sliding free of her with a reluctant shudder. On unsteady legs he rushed into the bathroom, slammed the door shut, and buried his face in his hands, calling himself a dozen kinds of idiot.

At least you didn't come in your pants. He snorted at that pathetic solace. Yeah, he'd managed to hold out for all of seven seconds. What a champ.

And now he was stuck in a bathroom with a window too small to crawl through, and he could never again walk out the door, even invisible, so… Yep. He'd have to stay here and die the undignified death he deserved. As long as he wore the necklace, no one would ever find him, right?

A soft knock startled him away from the door. "You okay in there?"

Mortified to realize he still had his pants down around his thighs, Beau hurriedly tucked himself back into some semblance of order, cinched his belt so tight it dug into his waist, and straightened his uniform as best as he could. "Uh, yeah. Fine."

"You don't sound fine."

The handle creaked down, and Beau leaped forward to slam the door as she tried to ease it open. Turned the key in the lock for good measure. Leaned his back against it just in case.

Lily sighed on the other side. "Are you freaking out because of what we did, where we did it, or how?"

"Yes," he answered. "Wait, no! What? I'm not freaking out! Can't a guy lock himself in the bathroom for a minute?" *Or forever…*

"Can you please come out and talk to me?"

Absolutely not. He could never face Lily Maverick again. Ever.

When he didn't actually answer, aside from vigorously shaking his head in the negative—which she couldn't see—Lily said, "Well, can you at least come out and lock yourself somewhere else? I have an appointment later tonight and I need the bathroom."

And there goes the last bit of dignity I used to possess.

Beau took off the invisibility necklace, stared at it for a moment before he pocketed it, and squared his shoulders. He'd never chickened out of anything in his life and he wasn't about to start now. Desperately clinging to that notion, he unlocked the door and pulled it open.

Lily stood there, wrapped in a silk robe, her hair mussed into a russet halo around her head, her jewel-bright eyes gazing up at him.

"Listen—"

"I'm sorry," he said, cutting her off. He owed her that much, at least.

But instead of the demure nod of acceptance he'd expected, Lily's expression turned thunderous, and she stomped her four-inch heel against the worn hardwood floor. "Will you stop that?"

Beau blinked. "Stop what?"

"Stop apologizing when you didn't do anything wrong. It's annoying."

"But I didn't even make you…you know."

She raised an eyebrow and supplied, "Come?" and Beau could have just died. Again. "First of all, you look a girl in the eye when you say stuff like that, not at the floor. Women respond to confidence. Use it if you got it, fake it if you don't. Number two, do I look like I need to rely on a man to get me off? No. Sex is a conversation, Beau. You don't *give* someone an orgasm, you help them *take* it. And in case it slipped your notice, I *did* come. Twice. Which is two more than I can say for any other virgin I'd ever been with. And C, don't lock a girl out of her own bathroom, man. That's just rude."

Without waiting for any kind of reply, she grabbed his hand and pulled him back into the bathroom, started the bathwater running, then dropped her robe and began working on the fastenings of his jerkin.

"What are you doing?"

"I'm taking a bath. And you're joining me."

"Err…"

She pulled the jerkin off him and reached for his shirt cuffs. "Don't mess with me, Legeare. You made me cranky, and you need to fix it."

"But—"

Yanking his shirt up and over his head, she demanded, "What did I just say?"

"I thought we agreed this would be on my terms! What happened to the customer always being right and all that crap?"

She snorted in answer, already working on his belt. He had to suck in his stomach so she could undo the clasp, and then his pants were down around his boots. He hadn't even taken off his boots. "That was for the first one. This one is for me. Boots. Off."

Beau complied, choosing to hop around as he did so, rather than sit down like a rational human being. "There," he declared when he'd finally gotten them free and tossed his clothes in the corner. "You happy?"

Lily smiled, blinding him with the brilliance of her sudden joy. "Thrilled," she replied, then took his hand again and pulled him to the bathtub. "In," she commanded.

Scowling, Beau turned off the water and stepped into it, wincing slightly at how hot it was. "Is this where you cook me alive for your midnight snack?"

"Oh, sweetheart, I'll get my midnight snack from you, don't you worry. But I prefer my meals fresh." She pushed him to lean back against the edge of the tub, then stepped in and settled between his legs with her back to his chest and her ass resting against his cock. Five minutes after it'd gotten its due, the damn thing twitched to rise again. Lily purred. "That's better." She relaxed back against him and sighed. "Now we can talk."

A hot bath had never felt so good. Now, if Beau would just unclench a bit, Lily might actually enjoy herself. She still couldn't believe how badly he'd freaked out. Guess she should have expected it, though. The man was simply too nice for his own good, always going out of his way to avoid hurting people, which in his case meant avoiding people, because why take the risk? Well, it was time for the turtle to come out of his shell.

Humming, more comfortable than she had any right to be, Lily reached for the soap bar and dipped it into the water. "You know what your problem is?" He tensed even more, going as hard as rock everywhere except where she wanted it. "You have no idea how amazing a lover you can be."

"I'm not sure that's a compliment," he groused, and without seeing his face, she knew he was blushing again.

"Then maybe you should let me finish." Taking his left hand in hers, she soaped it up and pressed his palm to her breast. As he'd done before, he instinctively squeezed her flesh just hard enough to stimulate without hurting her. He hefted the weight in his palm, then did a weird rolling thing like he was simulating a wave, which was oddly nice. And there went his thumb, rubbing over her nipple, back and forth, teasing zings of sensation out of her sensitive nerve endings.

That was the thing with Beau. He was inquisitive, and he learned *fast*. Now that he'd gotten that great, big elephant of his virginity out of the way, it seemed his aversion to touch would soon be a thing of the past. At least with her. Which, *Holy gods, yes please!*

Beau ran his knuckles along the underside of her breast, then trailed them up her cleavage, and briefly curled his fingers around her throat before returning to her breast—all things she adored and often demanded from her lovers. "You have this gorgeous body, and this amazing mind that thinks up so many…" Her breath caught when he pinched her nipple between his thumb and forefinger. Not with any kind of targeted intent, only with pure curiosity and a natural intuition so on point he could make a girl his willing slave with just those hands. "So many…different scenarios…"

Taking his other hand, she guided it between her legs. Didn't have to do much more than that. He'd already seen how she liked to be touched and didn't need to be told twice. He stroked his fore- and middle fingers up and down on either side of her clit, bringing them together on the downslide in the most delicious way. Lily arched, bringing her ass tighter against his cock, and it began to harden against her.

His hands stilled. "Are you faking right now?"

In answer, Lily tugged his fingers to the edge of her pussy where enough moisture had already gathered to make her slick. "Does this feel like I'm faking?" Without her having to say a word, he stroked a finger inside of her, hesitantly at first, then surer, deeper, guided by her body's responses. "See what you're doing right now?" she asked, finding it difficult to form words. It was ridiculous how easily he'd brought her to this state. "Do you have any idea how few men can do that?"

"What am I doing?"

His finger curled, the heel of his palm pressed against her clit, and Lily moaned, a mini-orgasm shivering through her abdomen. "Driving me crazy." She pulled his hand away, twisted around to face him. It took some creative maneuvering on her part to straddle his lap in the narrow tub, but somehow she managed, with Beau watching her in that earnest, baffled way that just made her want to eat him up. "You, Beau Legeare, are what we like to call a *natural*." She lowered herself onto his cock, slowly taking him as deep as she could, watching his face the entire time, loving the way his lids cast down and his pupils dilated. His jaw was clenched hard enough to make the muscles twitch, and she cupped his face between her hands. "Relax, darling, this is meant to be fun."

"I am relaxed," he grated between clenched teeth.

Lily smiled, kissed his jaw. "Trust me. Trust yourself. Think of this as a stealth assault mission."

Beau's eyebrows twitched down in a frown. The poor thing wasn't even breathing. And he needed to breathe.

Lily raised up, then slowly lowered herself back down, savoring the smooth glide of his cock inside her. Gods, he fit so well. Hard and hot, and thick enough to stretch her to her limits, just a hair's breadth from her pain threshold. *This man was made for me,* she thought, believing it on a level so deep, it seemed a fact of life. "You have a mission to make me come, and my entire body at your disposal to get it done. Just do what you always do." Up she went, squeezing him the whole way, then down to the hilt, memorizing the way his lips parted and his neck tensed, the way he stared straight into her eyes, as if he could see her soul in them. "Make a move." Up…and down.

Lack of oxygen forced him to release a small breath and gasp in more air. And then he held it again, making her grin in delight, even as she squeezed down hard on his cock, eliciting an almost pained groan. "Assess the situation." Up…and down. Rock back and forth. He was panting now, short, quiet breaths as if he didn't want the sound to distract him. "Strategize." Taking hold of his hands again, she placed them on her sides as she raised up, then she dug her fingers into his shoulders as she lowered down, leaning in to whisper against his lips, "And breathe."

She'd barely gotten the words out before he claimed her lips, devouring her again the way he had before, still as desperate, but now a little more controlled. Very little. Lily reveled in that unchecked wildness. He clutched her around the hips, holding her down on him before his hands cupped her ass, urging her up and down again in a rhythm he liked. And Beau liked it hard and fast.

Lily was more than happy to oblige, heedless of all the water splashing over the edge of the tub as she bounced up and down until the incandescence of another orgasm built at her core.

As if he felt her rising tension, Beau broke their kiss, stared at her face, then moved his hands, rubbing up her back on either side of her spine, then down her sides to her ass. He watched her reactions as he touched her and, meeting his gaze, Lily felt a brief stab of panic at the intensity of purpose she saw in his eyes. She'd presented him with a challenge, and now he wouldn't stop until he'd conquered it—and her. For Beau, it was a matter of honor to see the mission complete.

He might have been timid before, but this man was no one's lap dog. Already he was taking over, spiraling this thing between them way out of control, way too quickly, and she had neither the strength nor the desire to stop it. Beau pressed the pad of his thumb against her clit and rubbed a slow, torturous circle that had her crying out in a sudden, overwhelming, curl-your-toes and raise-your-hair full-body orgasm, and all she could think was, *Finally!*

Yet even as he rocked her through it, as Lily floated in momentary bliss, deep unease wormed its way into her heart. Because she now knew one thing with absolute certainty: Beau Legeare *would* make her a slave to his touch. Sooner, rather than later.

Lily shuddered in his arms, and Beau's balls pulled up tight. *Not yet!* Not again. He wanted to savor this as long as he could. Shoving his foot hard against the spigot, he focused on the cold metal digging into his sole and curled his hips back and forth, rocking into Lily as she came on him.

He understood now why Haig liked this so much. Watching Lily come apart was the most amazing thing he'd ever seen, and knowing he was the cause of it made him feel ten feet tall. As her pleasure eased off, she slumped against him and nuzzled into his neck, tickling him with her hair. "Go ahead," she purred. "Take what you need."

"Not yet," he managed to say, hissing an inhale when she curled her hips, rubbing herself against his groin as he thrust up. Beau clamped his arms around her, holding her in place as he pumped into her. Her breathing quickened, her nails digging into his back, and he sensed she was close again. The problem was, so was he. Clutching her hard, he pistoned his hips, needing to prove something—to Lily and to himself—but then she turned her head, licked up the column of his throat, caught his earlobe between her teeth, and he was a goner.

Biting down on her shoulder to muffle his shout, he came hard while she stroked his nape and clenched her muscles around him, milking more pleasure from him. He kept rocking his hips to prolong the pleasure, to get her there, too…somehow.

Somehow, he did. Lily moaned, clawing at him as she curled her hips against his. He felt her coming, and it was both a triumph and a relief. He wanted to roar his satisfaction, but all he could do was rub Lily's back and enjoy how good she felt draped all over him.

Overcome with lethargy, he went limp in the bathtub, head dropping back against the rim, but his arms refused to unlock, clutching Lily hard to his chest. He liked her there, far more than was wise. And what was worse, she didn't rush him, lying on him like a cat sunning itself on the rooftop.

"Why did you do it?" he asked hoarsely after he'd caught his breath. "Why push me like that?"

Lily sighed, stretched, then settled more comfortably against him. "Because you needed it. If I let you make the first move, we'd both be waiting for another ten years."

He chuckled. Probably true.

She levered herself away to look at him, and his skin screamed in protest at the loss of her warm weight. "Do you regret it?"

Beau brushed her hair behind her ear. "No," he answered. "I'm just wondering what happens now."

"Now," Lily replied, easing herself up and free of him, "I really need to get ready for my appointment. And you need to get started on whatever it is you came here to do."

Oh, shit. Beau blanched, casting far and wide for something to say.

Lily smiled a little, saving him from himself, even as she killed him. "It's okay, Beau. I'm not an idiot. I know you never would have come here if it weren't for some super-important mission for the queen." She leaned over to pull the plug so the bath could drain out, then took his hand and nudged him up and out of the tub. "But for what it's worth, I'm glad you came to me."

CHAPTER 5

"Are you okay? You seem a bit distracted."

"Hmm?" Lily blinked up at the tall, statuesque black beauty whose eyes had once been drunkenly described to her as "lambent pools of desire." Kendra and Lily were sharing this appointment, and they were both dressed for the part. Kendra's smoother-than-silk chocolate skin had been burnished with shimmery glitter lotion, her almond eyes adorned with golden eye liner. Her costume of a golden bikini was overlaid with a simple, white translucent sheath dress meant more to enhance her figure than to hide it. A golden circlet resting upon her long, straightened hair, Kendra, the royal desert queen was ready to hold court.

In contrast, Lily was supposed to be the clumsy milkmaid, with her hair in messy pigtails, her waist cinched super tight in a faux peasant corset that barely covered her areolas, and her ass peeking out from under a micro skirt. She'd sashayed out of the bathroom after getting ready, striking a pose for Beau, eager to see his eyes glaze over. Instead, his mouth had pressed tight in displeasure he'd valiantly tried to hide. She wouldn't lie, that had hurt a bit.

Worse, when Lily had asked him what was wrong, he'd answered, "Nothing. You look great. Have fun." And she couldn't even say he'd sulked. That hadn't been jealousy in his voice, just complete and utter disinterest. Ouch…

Kendra laughed. "What is with you today?"

"Nothing," she answered quickly. Too quickly. Rolling her shoulders to work out the tension in them, she took a deep breath. "I just have some things on my mind, that's all." Like the newly initiated Rebel hero currently sitting on her couch, scribbling things in the diary she'd received as a gift but never used—in freaking *code*.

Figures, the only way she could get Beau into her bed was by royal order. Double ouch…

"Well," Kendra said, flinging her hair over her shoulder to show off her golden choke collar, "whatever it is, put it *out* of your mind. We have a job to do here."

"Yeah, yeah." Like Mr. Jay would know the difference. He always paid for the full two hours and spent most of it trying to get it *back* up. "Ready when you are."

Kendra winked and opened the door, shoving her through into the scene. Lily pretended to stumble and fall onto her hands and knees. She whimpered a little, and immediately heard Mr. Jay gasp in delight.

His heavy breathing punctuated the silence as Lily got back up, wringing her hands as she faced Kendra. He was magically concealed behind an invisible screen that worked the same way as Beau's necklace. Neither Lily nor Kendra had ever actually seen Mr. Jay—he never participated in any sex going on during his sessions. No, Mr. Jay liked to watch, and he paid good money to have his fantasies acted out for his pleasure. At the moment, the sounds coming from behind that screen indicated he was already hard at work, pumping and squirming in the vibrating seat.

Kendra pulled Lily into her arms, kissed her dramatically, then yanked down Lily's corset and palmed her breast. "You've been a naughty girl, my dear. That batch of milk you spilled will cost us a week's supply of wheat."

Lily hung her head, even as she arched her back. "I'm sorry, my lady. You're right, I was very bad. I need to be punished."

"Get on your knees."

Mr. Jay's breathing quickened. He always came too quickly when Lily and Kendra played like this, which they all knew, but what the customer wanted, the customer got, so they kept on going. Sometimes he rebounded in time to get in one more O, and on those days, Lily always felt like she'd done a really good job. She liked to think that was the reason he kept coming back to her, even when there were a dozen other girls at his disposal.

Lily sank to her knees in front of Kendra, faking a gasp as Kendra play-grabbed her hair to tilt her head back. "Please, my lady." She kept her voice small, tremulous, and her breasts heaving with hard, fast breaths.

For a split second, an errant thought entered her mind. What if that was Beau watching her from behind that screen? Her body responded instantly to that idea, her pussy clenching desperately. Imagining him in the room, her eyelids grew heavy, her lips felt fuller, and her hands trembled—for real this time. Gods, just the thought of him was an aphrodisiac.

"Why are you stalling, girl?" Kendra demanded. "You know what to do."

Lily ran her hands up Kendra's legs from knee to hip. She caressed the swells of Kendra's ass, then hooked her fingers into the back of the thong and pulled it down. Would Beau like Kendra? She was beyond beautiful, an elegant creature, even without all of the makeup. Not like Lily's more down-to-earth, girl-next-door prettiness.

"Is that how you were taught to do it?" Kendra snapped.

Lily faked a flinch. "No, my lady."

"Then do it right!"

"Yes, my lady." Lily spread her knees, gyrating her hips for Mr. Jay's pleasure while she traced the inside of Kendra's thong string up to the waist, then around to the front. Once again, she tugged, and this time, Kendra allowed it to slip down past her knees.

Mr. Jay groaned. He was close.

If Beau had been there, he would have joined in by now. He'd have knelt behind her and kissed her neck, and fucked her while she fucked Kendra. And wow, did that fantasy do amazing things for her libido!

Deciding to prolong this a little, Lily sat back on her heels, wishing she was leaning against Beau, had his fingers in her pussy right now. "I can't, my lady. Please, don't make me."

Kendra play-hissed in displeasure. "You dare naysay me? Get on your hands and knees, peasant!"

Lily gasped. "No, my lady, please!"

"Do it!"

Biting her lower lip shyly, Lily turned away from Kendra and obeyed, spreading her knees and lifting up her ass, which pushed her skirt up to her waist. Her imagination added Beau beneath her, his face between her breasts, his hands on her ass. Oh yeah, she'd definitely need to get him in on this at some point.

"You will not make a sound," Kendra ordered.

Lily nodded, as if words were beyond her.

She felt Kendra's hand between her legs, stroking from her lower belly across her pussy in a long caress. Lily's body responded immediately, eager for stimulation of any kind, be it from a man or a woman. She wasn't picky.

Kendra pressed down on the center of Lily's back, forcing her to arch more, and Lily threw her head back, eyes closed and mouth open. "That's right," Kendra praised. "That's how a servant behaves."

Lily moaned. "Yes, my lady."

Kendra's hand landed on her ass. "I said be quiet!" She reached between Lily's legs again, and finger-fucked her hard and fast for a few seconds, bringing Lily to the very edge.

Lily squeaked, her breath quickening. Kendra was really good, but how much better would it have been with Beau instead?

Behind his magical screen, Mr. Jay stroked faster, panting like a dog after a hard run. He came before Lily did, yelling out a hoarse curse, then moaning in despair for having ruined it for himself yet again.

Lily smiled, winking at Kendra over her shoulder. In response, Kendra set back in, bringing Lily to a fast orgasm, and Lily cried out Mr. Jay's name. Before she'd come down all the way, Kendra rounded her and spread her legs, pulling Lily's mouth to her wet pussy.

When a bell chimed in the kitchen, Beau almost jumped out of his skin. He went to check it out and found a little green light glowing next to the dumbwaiter, a heavenly smell wafting out from its mysterious depths.

Dinner. Someone in the kitchens had sent up a full meal, complete with a small bottle of white wine, dessert, and an embossed little note with today's selection written out on it. Talk about five-star service. Had Lily ordered it, or was this how all of her meals were delivered? Either way, Miss Kiki sure knew how to treat her employees.

Beau took out the tray and carried it over to the little table by the window. Lily's room faced south, which guaranteed her views of the castle and the best natural light all day long. None of this surprised him, given that Lily's aunt was *the* Miss Kiki, the founder and proprietor of this establishment. What did surprise him was that the woman would allow her niece to follow in her footsteps.

When it came to Lily, Beau always found himself on an uncomfortable mental crossroads of need-to-know and please-don't-tell-me. Aside from the fact that he'd only lost his "V-card" a couple of hours ago, Beau didn't have any weird hang-ups about sex. His philosophy was, "To each their own, as long as all parties are willing." He had no issues with women or men selling their bodies, sharing partners, or anything like that in general.

But he'd known Lily since she was a teenager, and that was where his laid-back foundation of disinterest crumbled to pieces. He kept thinking of her the same way he had ten years ago: as a young girl in need of protection. Didn't matter that those times were long gone, or that she was a fully grown woman with a mind of her own, or that she had a vibrant sexual appetite and utilized it to make a living for herself—a really good living, by the looks of it. Every time he remembered her young, soot-smudged face, he kept thinking she was somehow trapped in this job.

Better get over that notion quick, sport. Lily Maverick is not a woman who will ever take that kind of shit from anyone, especially a man.

Heartfelt advice in the mental voice of Graeme Iskander. Beau would bet good money the man would laugh himself hoarse if he even suspected Beau's gallant thoughts about Lily. Misguided much?

Shaking his head at his own foolishness, Beau dug into the meal, not surprised that it tasted as good as it smelled. When he finished, he put the tray back in the dumbwaiter and flipped the switch to send it back down.

With the evening growing long, the brothel would be getting busy soon. Time for Beau to start working. He unlatched the bookcase and opened it just enough for him to squeeze through. Checking to make sure no one below had noticed, he made himself as comfortable as a man could get sitting on a glass balcony floor, and cleared his mind of anything to do with Lily Maverick and what she might be doing at this very moment.

By the time he'd actually managed that particular feat, he'd imagined Lily in a dozen different scenarios, with a dozen different people—including him—gotten up to pace three times, sat back down, and recited the Valefort Charter twice to get his hard-on under control. Now it was almost eight o'clock, the establishment was filling up, and Beau realized he'd missed at least seven people coming in and out.

Focus, dammit!

Beau shook his head hard and peered at the crowd below. Mostly commoners and tourists; no one he recognized. He watched the customers leer at the girls, watched how the girls worked the room, which people they favored with smiles and touches, and which ones they stayed away from.

Amalia, Jenna, and Lacie had what appeared to be regulars whom they greeted with a kiss and brief conversation before they led them to their seats. Monique, Olga, Tess, and Pru were new, not as aggressive as their mentors, but they used their shyness to connect with nervous tourists, make them more comfortable. Harley and Benna were the "hardcore chicks." They didn't mince words, and didn't bother with the timid ones, going instead for the rowdy group of drunks with grabby hands and their tongues practically lolling.

And then there were the good old boys: Peter, Michael, Jimmy,

Steve, and Erick. They weren't as hands-on as the girls, preferring to stay to the edges, available if needed, but somehow, without even trying, they always had at least one person at their side at all times, chatting, being friendly, and negotiating prices and services.

After a while, the crowd changed as new people replaced the ones who'd been satisfied and left. Still no possible suspects. Probably a slow night. Nothing had happened at the castle today, aside from Snow's audience with the Rebel Seven, and as far as Beau knew, no one had been appraised of those meetings. But there was a board meeting on the books for tomorrow.

When the massive grandfather clock in the common room struck one in the morning, Beau decided to call it a night. Only a handful of stragglers still left, anyway. He knew from Haig and Sebastian that the place never actually closed, but it got slow enough between midnight and noon that only two or three girls stuck it out, allowing the rest to get some sleep.

Satisfied that he wouldn't miss anything important, Beau decided to call it a night. He pushed to his feet, steadying himself against the wall until he regained feeling in his legs, then slipped back inside Lily's apartment and latched the bookcase closed.

"How'd it go?"

Startled, Beau spun around to face the cold fireplace between the living room and bedroom. Through the opening, he saw Lily, still wet from a recent shower and bundled in a fluffy robe, sitting cross-legged on the bed with a magazine in her lap and a box of take-out food on the night stand. "I thought you'd be asleep already." *Or with a customer.*

"Just got back." She'd said it with an easy smile as she forked a mouthful of noodles from the box. "Was too hungry to sleep, and apparently someone ate my dinner."

"Sorry about that," he said, ambling closer.

Lily shrugged. "S'okay," she mumbled, still chewing. "My fault, actually. I forgot to tell Cooke I'd need double rations. But I already sent her a memo, so there will be breakfast for two tomorrow."

"Thank you, that's very considerate."

She beamed. "My pleasure." How was she still so…perky? Beau

was exhausted.

"Well, uh… I guess I'm gonna call it a ni—"

"How did you end up in the Rebel Court?"

Brain slow to catch up, Beau replayed the last fifteen seconds in his head, trying to figure out what he'd said that could have logically led to a question like that. Nope. No connection. "What?"

"I'm just curious. I mean, we all heard the story about Graeme and Zorana's general, and Declan and Sebastian are pretty much legends. The others could easily have been promoted up through the ranks for their skills, but you… You were just a kid when the war began. You're the youngest of the Rebels, and physically the weakest—no offense—"

"None taken," he muttered. So he wasn't an overgrown behemoth bulging with layers of muscle. That didn't mean he was weak!

"—so how did you end up among them?"

She looked way too wired to drop this. With a weary sigh, he came in and straddled her vanity chair, resigned to his fate. "I used to steal food from Zorana's troops."

Lily choked on a bite of noodles. "Excuse me?"

Beau shrugged. "Times were tough; people didn't have much to share, and the places I used to beg from barely had enough to serve their paying customers. The only ones who were still well-fed and well-supplied were Zorana's troops. So I watched them for a while, learned their schedules, and then, you know… I took what I needed."

Lily stared at him, her fork hovering over the noodles.

Uncomfortable with her silence, he kept talking. "I got so good I could walk into a camp with fifteen soldiers hanging around, grab a satchel from the center table, and walk out without anyone ever seeing me. Except for Darius that one time. He saw me go in, watched me do my thing, grabbed me as I passed the wards, and dragged me straight to Graeme and the others."

Lily blinked slowly, her fork still hovering. She opened her mouth to say something, closed it, blinked again, then carefully set her food aside and turned to face him. "Why were you begging for food?"

Now it was Beau's turn to stare. How was *that* relevant to anything? "How do you mean?"

"I may have been a kid at the time, but I remember Kesteran just before the war. The troops were just being moved into those camps, and they never got fully settled before Snow's rebellion blew up in their faces. Even in places where they'd managed to get fully operational, every house still had rations coming in on a regular basis. So why did you have to beg?"

"Uh, because I didn't have a house. I was a street rat for as long as I can remember."

She gaped at him as if he'd grown another head. "Didn't you have any family who could take you in?"

Beau barked out a harsh laugh, but cut it short when Lily startled. Smoothing out his expression, he said, "I never knew my parents. The only family I had left was my aunt, and she had this bad habit of beating me off her stoop with a broom and threatening to kill me if I ever showed my face around her house again. So…that was kind of out."

She kept staring, and frankly there was only so much awkwardness Beau could take so, when it didn't look like she'd blink or close her mouth any time soon, he decided on a strategic retreat. "Well, good night, then." And because they'd never discussed sleeping arrangements, he turned off the living room lights and made himself comfortable on the couch. Soft seat cushions, a plush blanket draped over the back, a solid roof over his head, and indoor heating if it got cold? He'd slept in worse places.

What he didn't expect was to feel Lily quietly squeezing in beside him and resting her head against his chest.

Beau could say he hated it, but he'd be lying his street rat ass off.

CHAPTER 6

The dumbwaiter bell chime woke Lily out of a deep sleep and she began to stretch, only to be immediately brought up short in the very cramped space. And then her bed moved. "I think that's breakfast."

Lily tilted her head to seek out the source of that husky male voice and found Beau. Because apparently yesterday and last night hadn't been a dream. And there she was, lying on top of him like her own personal body pillow. Not that he seemed to mind. "Morning," he said, smiling.

At a loss for words, and still not fully awake, Lily replied, "Hi."

"Hungry?"

"I don't know yet."

"Got a busy day today?"

"Umm, I think I'm off, actually."

"Wanna have sex?"

"Okay."

Beau grinned and hiked her up higher on his body. But then he stopped, still holding her up, and frowned. "Should I be using condoms?"

For some reason, that struck Lily as absolutely hilarious. To spare his pride, she bit back her laugh, but couldn't help a tiny bit of sarcasm. "Normally, yes. Unless you know for a fact your partner is disease-free and using birth control, or you're both ready to have kids."

He scowled. "Har-har."

Lily grinned. "Don't worry. My aunt insists on all of her girls using birth control, and we each get a thorough physical once a month. Mine was last week. Clean bill of health. I can show you the certificate if you want."

She could practically see the decision trees forming in his head as he scanned her ears and throat, looking for an anti-pregnancy charm. To allay his curiosity, she held up her left hand, tapping her thumb against the thin platinum band on her pinky.

"Wow, that looks expensive."

"Miss Kiki pays well for quality. Necklace charms can get lost. Earrings can fall out. But a well-fitted, unobtrusive ring won't go anywhere, unless you decide to take it off."

"I didn't even notice it before." But now that he had, he took hold of her hand and peered at the band like it held all the secrets of the universe.

"That's the idea. The spell is engraved on the inside so it's always against my skin."

"Huh."

"Hey, can we talk about last night for a second?"

"Nope." Beau released her hand and leaned up to nuzzle the side of her neck while he pried at her knotted waist belt. He finally got it loose, and Lily sat up on him so he could take off her robe. Her flannel pajama top followed right after, and she shivered, her overheated skin prickling with goose bumps in the cool morning air.

His hands rubbed all over her, exploring her body in his Beau way, turning her on without any concentrated effort. Lily felt like a cat being petted into bliss—not an orgasm, though. Something deeper, much more satisfying. She wanted to purr. "I really think we should…discuss…"

He trailed his open mouth across her chest, one hand at the center of her back to hold her steady, the other sliding into the waist of her pajama bottoms to cup the curve of her ass. "Gods, that's nice." Her thigh muscles went taut, bringing her down harder on him. "But wait, hang on a second. Stop." Lily somehow managed to make herself pull his head away from her breast before he could latch on to her nipple and make her forget everything again.

His hands stilled at once, and he peered up at her. "Is something wrong?"

Dammit! Did he have to be so damn sweet? She could feel his erection all but twitching against her ass, his fingers curling to knead her ass as if he couldn't help himself—he had to be hard-up something awful—yet there he sat, waiting for her to give him the green light. And Lily would just bet if she told him to let go of her right now, he'd do it without question. Because Beau was just that kind of guy.

She looked into his eyes and hated to bring up a shitty past he probably didn't even want to acknowledge ever happened, but how could he have dropped that kind of bombshell on her with barely a shrug? *Yeah, I'm an orphan who grew up starving in the streets of Kesteran during the reign of the most oppressive, abusive ruler in the history of Valefort. Well, good night.*

Seriously?!

"I need to talk about this."

He frowned. "About what?"

"You! How did I never know all that about you? Do the other six know? Does Snow White? How are you not a totally unstable mess right now? What happened to your parents—and what the hell was wrong with your aunt? Why didn't anyone help you? What—"

Beau pinched her lips closed. "Good gods, woman, take a breath."

Still with the total calm! She wanted to kick him. Glaring daggers, she sucked in a deep breath, held it, then let it out. When he raised an eyebrow at her, she did it again, and one more time until Beau decided to release her. "I just need to know," she said.

His head tipped sideways. "Why?" She sensed there was a world of meaning behind that word, and a whole lot of implications she wasn't ready to face. Because she remembered one other thing from last night: Beau wasn't here for her; he was here on a royal mission, and when it was finished, he'd be gone again, and Lily wasn't sure anymore she could handle that.

"Because," she began, with no clue how to finish the sentence. Then her eyes began to water. *No, no, no! Don't you dare cry!* There was no faster way to send a man running for the hills. *Oh my gods, stop freaking crying!* Biting down on the inside of her cheek as hard as she could without drawing blood, she turned away and faked a sneeze, quickly dashing the offensive, salty moisture away.

If Beau noticed her temporary break with sanity, he didn't comment on it. "Okay," he said, kissing her shoulder before he handed back her pajama top. After she put it on, his arms came around her again, and he swung his legs off the couch and stood, still holding Lily. "But breakfast first."

As she'd requested, two breakfast trays waited inside the dumb-waiter: Cooke's signature waffle feast, complete with a pile of bacon, soft-boiled eggs, apple cider, and a berry salad. They each took their own and set them on the table, but when Lily reached for her chair to sit, Beau pulled her back into his lap.

"I don't talk about my past, because I don't see the point," he said, taking a strip of bacon to chew on. No sweet tooth. Noted. "I never thought of my childhood as lacking; never knew I was missing anything, you know?"

"You never looked at other kids and wished you had what they had?"

"Like what?" Gods, he wasn't faking that nonchalance! He really *didn't* see anything wrong with his childhood.

To give herself a second to absorb this, Lily poured enough maple syrup on her waffles to soak them into a goopy mess, then picked up her fork. "A home, toys, warm food, school, family, I could literally go on for hours. How could you not have wanted all that?"

He was quiet for a while, seeming to think it over, then he said, "It wasn't really that bad. I lived in this little burrow under the Kissing Bridge. It was warm enough most of the year. I had an old mattress someone had outgrown, a little oil lamp for light, and one of those plastic under-bed storage boxes for my things.

"I'd hang around the baker's back door in the early mornings to get the first batch of bread that he usually burned, so I had something warm in my belly to tide me over for the rest of the day. After that,

I'd go sit outside the school window and listen to the kids sound out their lessons. I'd share lunch with Old Peg at O'Malley's Pub and talk to her for a few minutes before she had to go back to work.

"In the afternoon, I'd keep to the shopping strip. I could usually get enough coins from rich ladies to buy myself dinner, sometimes even a pair of socks, or a wool cap when it got cold. I learned from old books people left out on the curb, I amused myself fixing broken toys they left lying in the park. Before I grew too big, I used to be able to sneak into the theater for a movie or a play. Honestly, until Zorana started restricting magic and forcing people into poverty, I had everything I needed."

"Except family," she said softly.

"I did have my batty aunt Elsa."

When she didn't laugh with him, he sobered. "Snow and the other six are my family."

And that right there explained absolutely everything about Beau Legeare.

"What about when winter came? You had to be freezing in a little hole in the ground burrow."

She seriously wasn't letting this go. Why? Beau knew she was a kind, personable woman, but this went beyond normal curiosity. He didn't want her pity; didn't want her looking at him differently because he might or might not have dined on decomposing fish and roadkill once or twice. He didn't want her thinking about him having to learn to be sneakier than everyone else because, as the runt of the town, the bigger street kids would beat him until he passed out if they caught him stealing in their turf.

No point to any of that now. He'd made his peace with it all years ago when Saxon had returned from a raid one night with a fur coat for Beau because "you always look so cold it makes *me* shiver." In that moment Beau had realized that if he hadn't been orphaned and abandoned, he'd never have learned what he could do; would never have crossed paths with Darius; would never have met Graeme, and Snow, and the others; would never have looked at a battlefield map and strategized Snow's rebellion, eventually winning the civil war.

And he never would have met Lily.

So instead of answering her question, he asked one of his own: "How did you end up working for your aunt?"

Lily scowled at him over her shoulder. "I see what you're doing." Then she faced forward again and rearranged the plates on her tray. "But I'll let it slide for now, because that is actually a funny story." She spooned up a morsel of syrupy goop and held it up for him to taste. Beau took it, but couldn't prevent a sour grimace. So much sugar. *Ugh.* Lily laughed. "Definitely not a sweet tooth. Got it." She leaned back against him and made herself comfortable, which meant his arms decided to circle her waist and his chin rested against her shoulder.

"Once upon a time, there was a sweet little girl whose parents died in a car crash."

"I read about that on an old news site. I'm sorry."

"It's okay. It was a long time ago. Unlike your aunt, mine was kooky, but she still loved me and took me in. I grew up in this place; had all the girls doting on me, all the servants playing with me, sneaking me cookies and teaching me things a young girl probably shouldn't know. I was never lonely. Not for one single instant in my entire life."

Lucky girl.

"Then Zorana gave her army free reign and everything went to hell. I would hear them come in at night, and my aunt would try to sweet talk them into spirits and food. Both were drugged to make the soldiers mellow so they wouldn't hurt the girls *too* much. But they found out eventually. The squad captain threw a huge fit and decided to burn us all out. That was the night Haig and his friends saved us and brought us to the mine.

"Anyway, the point is, sex was never a mystery to me, but I don't think it really hit home for me or my aunt until the night of my sixteenth."

That would have been a year or so after Miss Kiki moved them all out of the mine and to a temporary home deep in the Elderwood.

"What happened then?"

"I had a date with a boy to lose my virginity. He was a few years older, already been around the block a few times, so I figured he'd know what he was doing. Yeah, turned out, not so much. And he didn't really take it well when I told him so."

Beau chuckled. "Hurt his pride?"

"I think I must have. He left red-faced before he even got my pants off. My aunt had a field day with that. After she finally stopped laughing, she called in one of the boys she'd just hired to do the deed proper."

"And did he?"

"Oh, yes."

He was glad Lily couldn't see him scowl at that.

"But as an unintended side effect, he made it so good, my aunt looked at me the next day and said, 'Sweet mercy, girl, you're going to be all kinds of trouble now, aren't you?' And since she has no patience for troublesome girls, she gave me a choice: Work a summer for her, safely and responsibly, to get it out of my system, or take my chances on my own. But she made it clear if I went off on my own and got myself sick, pregnant, beaten, or killed, she wouldn't lift a finger for me."

"That sounds kind of harsh."

"Not really. She made it an easy choice. I was getting bitch-slapped by wave after wave of crazy hormones so hard I would have taken lovers, regardless, but at least working for my aunt, I had her and all the other girls looking out for me. They sent me to boys and young men I could handle, they taught me how to keep myself safe, had a healer in the wings just in case, and any time I got a bad feeling about a client, they let me walk away, no questions asked. I worked out that summer, and afterward marched into Aunt Kiki's office and negotiated myself a contract."

"What about school?"

"Private tutors—old female ones with no interest in any kind of sexual bribery. Technically, I have a four-year college education in kinesiology and physical therapy. I just don't have a degree to show for it." She twisted to glance at him from the corner of her eye. "Are you surprised? Have I shocked you with my love of sex and utter disinterest in abandoning my hedonistic lifestyle—or the fact that I know what 'hedonistic' means and how to use it in a sentence?"

"No."

She twisted around farther. "You're not going to tell me I'm wasting my potential, or try to save me from myself?"

Beau shrugged. "Do you need saving?"

"No."

"There you go."

Lily stared at him for a moment, then shrugged and picked up her fork. "Fair enough."

CHAPTER 7

"Give those back!"

Lily squealed, leaping onto and over the bed to get away from him. "No way!"

"Dammit, Lily, will you stop?"

When he came after her, she dashed around the foot of the bed, racing into the bathroom, his clothes clutched tight to her chest. Beau's foot caught in the bedsheets and he fell hard enough against the wall to make her wince, but she wasn't giving up. With a defiant jerk of her chin, she opened the laundry chute.

He straightened slowly, an ominous glower sending a shiver down her back. "Let's not be hasty, here. I'm sure we can work something out."

"You are *not* wearing the same set of clothes for a week without washing them. I won't let you."

Beau approached the bathroom, deliciously naked from their morning fuck session, trying to look tough, but all it did was make Lily horny. Again. Beau was quickly becoming her own personal drug—and how was that fair? "I won't argue that," he said in his best, negotiator voice. "But I can wash them in the sink on my—*gods dammit, woman!*"

Lily slammed the chute door closed before he could reach into it to try to pull his clothes back out. Wash them in the sink… Where did he think he was?

Beau banged his head against the wall. "I can't believe you did that."

"Will you relax? You'll get your clothes back tomorrow morning, professionally laundered and pressed."

"And what am I supposed to wear in the meantime?"

She smiled sweetly in the face of his rage. "I could get you something, but I guarantee you wouldn't like it." Given that the only clothes his size would be costumes, she felt pretty confident he wouldn't touch them with a ten foot pole. And wasn't that a shame? "What's wrong with staying naked for a day? Don't tell me you've never done that before."

"Of course not!"

Crossing her arms beneath her breasts, Lily cocked her hip. "You know, the more I learn about you, the more I realize how much you need me in your life."

Beau heaved a sigh worthy of a grieving widow. "Lily, I have work to do here, and I can't sit out on your balcony naked while I do it."

"Hello! Invisibility charm." When he glared at her, she shrugged. "Or you can give it a rest for one night and work on me instead."

"Is that right?"

Yes, please! She nodded, putting on her innocent face. "'Fraid there's not much else to do around here. The TV only gets local channels, I don't have any books, and the only games I know how to play are naughty ones."

"Good thing I'm a resourceful kind of guy."

Lily clasped her hands behind her back, turned her heel outward, and blinked up at him from beneath her lashes. "So what do you want to do?"

The best part about keeping Beau naked was getting to watch him rise to the occasion. "I think I'll start at your toes," he mused. "Then maybe work my way up. At least halfway. That should keep me busy for a while."

"If you're sure…"

"Oh, I'm sure."

With a regretful sigh, she shuffled her feet back to the bed. "The customer wants, the customer gets." She tugged the covers off, then laid down spread-eagle. "Do your worst, sir." She squeezed her eyes shut for good measure, but inside she was dying to see him.

She never heard him approach, but then he grasped her right ankle and raised it up. "You have the cutest little toes. I could just eat them up." His mouth closed on her big toe, teeth lightly scraping as he hollowed his cheeks and sucked. Lily bit back a smile, still keeping her eyes closed. Who knew the straight-laced rebel had a kinky side?

He kissed her instep, licked a circle around her ankle, then massaged up her calf as his mouth trailed across her skin, leaving a hot, moist trail in its wake. The mattress depressed as he climbed on, still kissing her legs, and by the time he'd reached her knee, she wanted to squirm. When he lapped at the back crease, Lily squeaked, and he did it again, reaching for her other leg at the same time to tease the same spot there with his fingers.

Lily's toes curled, her breaths came quicker. "Beau…"

She felt him smile against her inner thigh, just above her knee. "Noted," he murmured, then nuzzled his way up her inner thigh while he continued to play with her knees, the backs of her thighs. Settling between her legs, he lifted them over his shoulders, still massaging up to her ass and hips as his mouth *slooooooowly* inched up.

Sweet gods, it took all Lily had not to grab him by the hair and force his mouth where she needed it. But this was Beau's first time eating pussy, and he needed to do this at his own pace. He probably didn't even realize what his teasing was doing to her. Or did he?

Lily cracked open one eye and looked down to find him watching her with an almost unnerving focus. He pressed a kiss to one side of her sex and his mouth brushed ever so lightly across her clit as he turned to press another to the other side. Lily's hips almost came off the bed, and his eyes sparked dangerously. "Noted." Oh yes. He knew exactly what he was doing, and he liked it.

"Beau, please," she panted and, for perhaps the first time in her life, actually meant it.

"What do you want me to do, Lily? Tell me what you need."

"My clit. Please, I need your mouth on my—*yes!*" He took her flesh between his lips, sucked the way he had her toe. Pulling away, he let it slide free, then came back for another open-mouthed kiss, pressing his tongue flat against it. "Oh my gods, that's it. More! Please, Beau, I'm so close."

He pulled back again to nuzzle her inner thigh. "Not yet."

Breath left her. "What? Why?"

"Because I'm not finished with you." To prove his point, he tilted her hips up higher and delved his tongue into her pussy.

Lily cried out his name, fisting the sheets so hard, threads popped beneath her nails. Beau didn't ask if she was faking again; her body's every twitch and tremor would be obvious to him with his hands splayed on her abdomen. Her heels dug into his back, and his arms around her legs tightened to keep her still as his tongue speared into her, and his mouth made smacking noises against her flesh. "More!" she pleaded, and he gave her more, with his fingers thrusting in to replace his tongue and his mouth back at her clit. "Gods yes! Turn your fingers up—*ah, yes,* like that. Harder. Yes… Yes, yesyes*yes!*"

Lily grabbed his hair, gyrated her hips as she came, and Beau grinned, loving this sight of her. He thumbed her clit, varying the pressure until he found one that stilled her hips, and she relaxed her hold on him, letting him bring her through it.

She kept humming her pleasure even after she released him and melted limp on the bed. If she were a cat, she'd be purring up a storm.

"I like this," he decided.

Lily smiled. "Oh baby, then you're going to *love* this next part." She sat up and pulled him fully onto the bed; kissed him deep as her hands smoothed down his front, and then her mouth followed the same path down to his cock. "I'm betting this is feeling in some sore need of relief right about now."

It bobbed in answer and his entire body tensed, anticipation coiling until he thought he'd explode. His lungs burned, heart thrashing, but he didn't dare take a deeper breath for fear he might say something wrong, do something to scare her. Like grab her hair and force her mouth on him.

Thankfully, Lily didn't make him wait long. She grabbed his cock at the base, squeezed as she looked him up and down. "So hard." Her hand moved up and all the way off over the head, and Beau's eyes briefly rolled back. He wouldn't last long at this rate. As if she'd read his mind, she gazed up into his face and said, "Hold out as long as you can."

She licked her lips and took him in her mouth. All the way to the base. Beau gasped out a curse, fisting her hair, but released her immediately. She winked up at him, reached for his hands and put them back on her head. *You can do this*, he told himself. *Have some fucking self-control, dammit!* Raking his shaky hands through her hair, he pulled it back so he could see her better. Her tongue lapped at him as she pulled back, lips sealing around the head before she sucked hard, taking him right back in again.

Beau groaned, digging his heels into the mattress to keep his hips from thrusting up. "Fuck."

She took him in again, and one more time, then let his cock pop free of her mouth, pumping him with her hand. "You like that?"

He couldn't answer. Partly because he couldn't find his voice, but mostly because he feared if he did right now, he'd only be able to say, "Marry me." Instead, he pulled on her hair to signal he wanted her back.

Lily chuckled and set back in, and this time he couldn't keep his hips still. She didn't seem to mind, held still and hummed, the flat of her tongue lapping at him as he thrust into the wet heat of her mouth, and he was so close it hurt. But he didn't want this alone. "Touch yourself," he said heat flooding up his cheeks. "Make yourself come."

She reached down at once, and even though he couldn't see her hand working at her pussy, he watched her eyes grow heavy-lidded, felt her mouth go just a little slack on him as she worked her own flesh right along with his. She hummed louder, the vibrations of her voice intensifying that twisting thing she did with her hand at the base of his cock as she sucked the tip hard.

Beau's head fell back, and he had no hope of tempering his pleasured shout. She whimpered around him, her hand pumping harder, faster, and Beau wanted to tell her to stop, that he was about to come, but then her other hand, still wet with her own juices, fondled his balls and he couldn't do anything except shout her name as he came.

And Lily didn't pull away. She took all of him, sucked and licked him clean, swallowed him down, then shifted up to his stomach and collapsed there. That's where they stayed, spent and boneless, with only their breaths breaking the silence, until the dumbwaiter chimed to signal dinner.

CHAPTER 8

That night was another dismal bust of watching Miss Kiki's earn ducats hand over fist, without any sign of suspicious activity from patrons or employees. He'd received an email memo from Snow's secretary earlier with a recap of the board meeting, scanned it briefly, but hadn't seen anything that might be useful to a detractor. The economy was strong; the magic-refining business was booming, and Snow's social initiatives were finally producing tangible results.

Valefort was experiencing massive economic growth, something they all sorely needed after the war. Even faraway districts in the Elderwood and the northern White Plains were benefiting from more accessible, affordable magic. Difficult to believe anyone would have a problem with the way Snow ran things. Of course, there would always be those for whom greater equality meant less power and prestige, and those who just plain hated Snow White because she wasn't Zorana.

The clock struck one, and once again Beau slipped back into Lily's apartment without anything to show for the ass-numbing hours he'd spent on the glass balcony. Hopefully something would shake loose tomorrow.

It didn't.

Not a hint of a conspiracy all night, or the next night, or the next. Six whole days and nights gone, with absolutely no progress. Beau was beginning to think he was wasting time that was quickly running out. He'd negotiated a week here with Lily in the hopes that it'd be enough time to learn what he needed, report to Snow, and get back to his normal duties. But then, Beau didn't have his Network feeding him intel here.

At noon on the seventh day, Beau received an email notification on his phone. Subject: Progress Report. The body was blank, but bore Snow White's royal seal in the signature line. She was getting impatient, and she probably had good reason.

Making sure the connection was secure, he replied, "No activity. Require incentive for contact. Please advise."

Her response was immediate. "Calling emergency board meeting for tomorrow. One chance."

Beau sat back. This could get them what they needed, or tip their hand and put Snow and her entire regime at risk. One chance was right; Beau couldn't afford to screw this up.

With Lily out at an appointment, he had a few hours to think before she returned. The next few days would be crucial, and as much as he hated to admit it, he couldn't do it on his own. In his head, he quickly ran through the roster and determined four of his people were at his immediate disposal, with an additional two who could be pulled from other assignments if necessary, and three informants whom he could utilize if he could guarantee their anonymity. In his line of work, that was a veritable army.

But it wasn't enough.

He needed someone on the inside. Someone low-profile, with access to restricted areas, who could freely move about without raising suspicion.

Two hours later, his phone pinged again. Snow's secretary had sent a group email to the board members, summoning them to an unscheduled meeting at three o'clock tomorrow to discuss a new acquisition possibility for Valeguard Industries, Inc. A second email followed shortly thereafter from Snow herself, addressed to him alone, with an attachment outlining a shell company Beau himself had put together.

She had an entire database of them to use at her discretion. None of them existed, except on paper, but on that paper, those companies looked so real, if someone were to leak one, it'd have a thousand investors by end of business day.

Yeah, he was that good.

The one Snow had chosen was a hypothetical manufacturer of a nonexistent valve that would make it possible for refined magic to be delivered through pipelines like water or gas. A possible game changer for the industry, or the perfect opportunity for a traitor to swipe it out from under Snow, along with her market share and crown.

The game was on.

I'm in love with Beau Legeare.

Not something Lily should have been thinking about before a staff meeting, but there it was. She couldn't *stop* thinking it. Somewhere in the last few days, her mission to make Beau fall in love with her had backfired something awful.

I am so screwed...

And not in a good way.

Miss Kiki made her entrance through the secret door that connected the lounge with her office. As usual, when conducting business, she was dressed in a conservative white skirt suit with nothing but a black lace bra beneath the jacket. Her graying hair was pinned up in a bun, a single curl left loose to fall over her face and her sexy vintage glasses. She looked like a horny student's wet dream, an image she fiercely protected at all times. No one ever saw her with her hair down unless they were paying for the privilege.

"All right, let's cut the chatter," she said, and the room quieted instantly. Splitting her stack of portfolio folders, she gave one half to Erick by the door and the other to Lacie on the other side of the room. "Pass those out, please. I expect you all to have them memorized by tomorrow."

Shoving all thought of sweet, courteous, amazing-in-bed Beau out of her mind, Lily got her copy and passed the rest on to Kendra.

"We finally have the theme for our annual masquerade ball: Midnight Magic. The planning committee has put together the staging and the menu, and you will each have a choice of costumes to wear for the occasion. We will *not* be repeating last year's embarrassment; there will be no last-minute costume swaps, so I don't want to hear any whining when you decide your mermaid outfit makes it impossible to access your 'happy place.' I'm talking to you, Amalia."

The group chuckled goodnaturedly, but most of them were too busy leafing through the program to pay too much attention.

"Your selection is due by midnight tomorrow, and you'll be scheduled for two fittings before the event. Make use of them. That's an order."

Lily admired the elegant invitation for a moment before she turned her attention to the program. The annual ball was a favorite at Miss Kiki's for both employees and clients. On that day, the brothel would be transformed into a magical wonderland with special stages and acts, and just one simple rule: No such thing as a private appointment.

Miss Kiki's crown achievement was her ability to strip inhibitions and create a free-flowing orgy so popular, people from all walks of life went to extreme measures to secure an invitation. Of course, they always failed. The masquerade guest list was exclusive, and exclusively at Miss Kiki's discretion.

"Any questions?"

Several hands went up, and Miss Kiki spent the next forty minutes addressing their comments. Not bothering to listen in, Lily leafed through the portfolio, scanning through the schedule of acts only long enough to see that she wouldn't have one of her own this year. Instead, she, Kendra, and Michael would be sharing the dryad glen room. Their job would be to get the orgy started and keep it going whenever the action stalled. It'd be a long, intense assignment, but luckily her aunt had chosen Lily's partners well. They'd done this before and knew how to read each other so they could take breaks at intervals and step in when one of them flagged.

Lily skipped forward to the decor section. The sketches looked duly impressive, with hanging ribbons and curtains of the softest gossamer, green-and-blue body pillows, and the in-floor pool transformed into a magical lagoon. She was so absorbed in the images, she didn't notice the meeting was over until two dozen chairs suddenly scraped across the floor as everyone rushed off to pair up with their partners and go over costume selections. Michael waved from across the room to acknowledge Lily and Kendra, but there were too many people milling around for him to make it toward them.

Then Miss Kiki herself was there, looking at Lily over the top of her glasses. "Lily, a word, please."

Because her aunt hadn't waited for a response before walking off, Lily rushed to follow her into her office.

"Have a seat."

Miss Kiki didn't believe in corporate hierarchies. Instead of a suite of desks and power chairs, her office was set up like a cozy library with a set of couches and love seats arranged around a large coffee table. Her favorite armchair was off limits, so Lily sat on the couch instead, crossing her ankles and resting her hands on her knees like a schoolgirl.

"Is there anything you want to tell me?" her aunt asked.

Lily frowned. "About what?"

Miss Kiki sat on the edge of the coffee table. "Let's start with the double rations you've requested from Cooke a few days ago."

"Meals are deducted from my salary, so it's not like I'm stealing."

"You know that's not what I meant."

"What did you mean, Aunt Tabitha?"

Lips pressed into a thin line, Tabitha Maverick took off the glasses she didn't really need, then pulled the pins out of her hair, shedding her naughty teacher persona. Age had faded the russet curls into a unique blend of gray and honey brown, but they were still as thick and vibrant as they'd been in her youth. "I just mean I'm concerned that you might be keeping something—or some*one*—from me."

Shit. "Has there been a complaint about my appearance or performance?"

"No, but—"

"Have I missed any appointments, arrived late, or finished too early?"

"No. Still—"

"Still, nothing. I am my own person, I have my own life, and I don't need to explain anything—or any*one*—about it to you. So unless someone has submitted a complaint, the amount of food I choose to order or for whom is really none of your business."

Aunt Tabitha studied her for a moment with a penetrating gaze that'd made many an employee crack in the past. Lily stared right back. "Is that your final word on the matter?" Tabitha was an absolute doll most of the time, but she had an unpleasant habit of not respecting boundaries. Give her an inch, and she'd take over your entire life. Lily would never let that happen. Especially if it jeopardized Beau's mission.

"It is," Lily confirmed.

Aunt Tabitha nodded slowly, just once, never breaking her stare. "Very well. Your life, your choice. But don't forget the house rules. You break them, and you'll be living that life of yours somewhere else. Do I make myself understood?"

"Don't worry, Aunt, I have no intention of breaking your rules." *On purpose.* Miss Kiki's had a plethora of guidelines for employees to follow, but only three ironclad rules, the breaking of which resulted in immediate dismissal and loss of pension benefits: No pregnancies. No client stealing. And no lovers, boyfriends, or husbands allowed in the establishment. Which meant she was hanging on by a technicality. "So, are we finished?"

"For the moment."

"Then I wish you a good evening, Aunt."

"And you, niece."

CHAPTER 9

And look at the swatches! Have you ever felt anything so soft before in your life? Next week can't get here fast enough!"

Beau hummed in answer without sparing her a glance. He hadn't said a single word since greeting her when she'd come in before dinner, and that had been barely a hello.

Lily closed the portfolio and pushed it to the very edge of the table. Then she clasped her hands together and waited. And waited. And the longer she waited, the more worked up she got, until her foot started bouncing, knocking her knee against the table's underside.

When the silverware started rattling, Beau finally noticed and looked up. "Are you okay?"

"You tell me," she replied. "Have you heard a single thing I said to you?"

"Of course."

"Really? Repeat it back to me."

Beau blinked at her, then sighed. "I'm sorry. I've just got a lot on my mind today, that's all."

"Must be serious." It wasn't only his lack of voicing coherent sentences; he hadn't made a pass at her, either. Lily had gotten used to him waiting for her as soon as she got out of the shower when she got home each night. He might spend hours sitting out on her balcony, but he never went out there before giving her a *proper* greeting with a few Os and a shared dinner. It was almost domestic that way, and he never seemed to care that she might have just been with someone else, which made it so much harder for Lily to keep some semblance of an emotional distance. Would any other man be as accepting of what she did? "You want to talk about it?"

"More than you'll ever know. But I can't."

"Because you don't trust me?"

He sat back. "That's not fair."

"Maybe not, but it's true, isn't it?"

"Come on, Lily, you know what I do. I *can't* trust *anyone*."

"And you enjoy living that way? Doing this spy shit, day in and day out, all alone?"

"What should I do instead? Fuck a bunch of strangers out of their money?" He swore, instantly contrite. "That was out of line. I'm sorry. I didn't mean it."

Maybe not. Maybe it was just his frustration talking. But Beau was first and foremost a genius tactician and a master strategist. He could literally use words as weapons, and until this moment Lily hadn't realized how dangerous that was; how much he always held back to keep from hurting people.

He might not have done it on purpose, but that didn't change the fact that he'd managed to say the one thing guaranteed to hurt her the deepest. It didn't make that lump in her throat any smaller, or her breath come easier, or her chest ache less to know that he was just doing what came to him naturally. Like when she made him see stars with just her hand, or deep-throated him into oblivion.

Hell of a wake up call.

Lily Louise Maverick, you are such a romantic idiot.

She clenched her hands together so hard, her knuckles stood out stark white. She stared at Beau's open collar, because if she looked at his face right now, she'd say something they'd both regret. And all the while she tried so hard to remind herself that this was all just a really long transaction. Lily was getting paid to provide a service, and it didn't include illusions of domesticity or emotional hissy fits.

Beau leaned forward, reached for her hands. "Lily, I'm really sorry. Please don't—"

She jerked away before he could make contact. If he touched her, she'd fold like a cheap card trick. Pushing away from the table, she picked up her portfolio in one hand and her plate in the other. "Good luck with your mission tonight."

Lily slammed the bedroom door behind her and slid the metal screen across her side of the open fireplace, closing herself off completely.

Beau buried his face in his hands. *That went fucking well. Award winning performance. Stellar technique, Legeare. Way to make the sweetest woman in the world hate your fucking guts.*

He had to fix this. Somehow…

His phone beeped multiple times with incoming messages. Beau scanned through them, memorizing their content before wiping them from the phone's memory. Three of his men were in place around Miss Kiki's, with two more on the way to their designated locations. He'd ordered them to surround the establishment at a distance and to monitor all paths leading to it. Because none of them knew what they were looking for, all of them were instructed to keep their phones on at all times and wait for word from Beau.

He'd thought about getting a man down into the common room, too, but ultimately decided it'd be too risky.

That left Beau on another six-hour watch on Lily's balcony. And it was almost showtime.

This was not the way he'd planned to spend his last night here.

Resigned to his sad, lonely fate, Beau straightened up the living room, put on the invisibility necklace, and shuffled out onto that balcony.

His heart wasn't in it tonight. He noted the regulars, but the new faces blended together until he lost track of how many had come and gone. Miss Kiki's was bustling with people tonight and even the good old boys were kept busy carrying on multiple conversations at the same time. Three separate lap dances in progress, one of them crossing the line from lap dance to actual sex. No one seemed to care.

Then, just before midnight, a young man slammed his tankard of ale down onto the table, pushed to his feet, and demanded, "Let's see what's on the menu tonight!"

Obnoxious didn't even begin to describe it. Beau rolled his eyes as the guy wriggled his fingers at the girls, beckoning them closer. They kept their smiles in place, swished their hips gamely as they lined up in front of him, but Beau had watched them long enough now to know they were not happy to be treated like cheap goods.

"Twirl around for me, beautiful," the guy said to Amalia on the far left. She turned her back to him, paused for a second, and turned back. "Mmm, lovely. Now you, sweetheart," he motioned to Lacie, who copied Amalia. Down the line he went, ogling each girl until he got to Harley. "Show me the goods, baby."

And Harley put her hands on her hips and said, "Make me."

The crowd hooted, and Beau allowed himself a smirk. When Harley really dipped into her mean streak, like she seemed to be doing now, she would provoke a guy and then verbally emasculate him with a viciousness that made Beau cringe.

Not surprisingly, the young pup moved on to the next girl.

By now, he had everyone's attention, and once he'd thoroughly inspected each girl, he stepped back and tapped his chin, appearing to deliberate a weighty matter. For some reason, something about him struck Beau as odd. Average height, messy brown hair, disheveled clothes—but they were nice clothes, good quality, and though his boots were scuffed, Beau could see the signature clasp of a high-end shoemaker on the side.

He tried to recall when the youth had come in. Couldn't have been too long ago; his tankard was still almost full. He walked up and down the line of girls, and Beau felt the tension in the room escalate higher the longer he took to decide. Taking a chance, Beau pushed to his feet and slipped back inside.

He took off the necklace in front of Lily's door, then knocked.

No answer.

"Lily, are you asleep?"

Silence.

"I need you to come out. Please. It's an emergency."

Just as he was about to knock again, she opened the door. "What do you want?"

To take you back to that bed and keep you there until your eyes sparkle again. "I need you to come take a look at something."

She scowled. "If you're worried about that little birthmark on your right ass cheek, call a healer. I'm going back to sleep."

"No, wait!" Beau slapped his hand against the door before she could slam it in his face. "I know I screwed up, okay? I promise I'll find a way to make it up to you, but right now I need you to identify someone in the common room."

She hesitated, looking over his shoulder, then back at her bed. "Is this a trick?"

Running out of time! "No trick, I swear. But we don't have much time. Here, put this on." He hung the necklace around her neck and pulled her across the living room to the bookcase doorway. Back against the wall right next to it, he took a quick glance outside, then nudged her through and said, "See that guy pawing Tess?"

"Mister Menu? Yeah. What about him?"

"Does he come in a lot?"

"Not too often. But he always does that; makes us into a cheap, roadside attraction until he gets the others so riled up, someone snaps."

Down below, a pot-bellied, bald man with massive sideburns and his stained shirt open to the waist threw a chicken leg at the youth. "Fucking choose already! I don't come here to watch a line-up. Asshole."

Looking smug enough to earn a beating, Mister Menu crooked his finger at Amalia and yanked her against him, effectively releasing the other girls to return to whatever they'd been doing before.

"And that's our Wednesday night entertainment," Lily said. "Anything else?"

Beau didn't answer at first, too busy watching the crowd. It probably wouldn't have been obvious to anyone except Beau, but as soon as he saw it, Beau pulled out his phone and typed out a blast message to his people: *Two pigeons roosted on the fountain at noon. The brown had a broken wing. The yellow was missing a foot.*

"What does that mean?"

Beau jerked back. He hadn't realized Lily, still invisible, was now standing beside him, watching him send the message to his men. "I don't know," he said, wide awake and more alert than he'd felt all day.

"Right," she retorted. "Got it." She pulled off the necklace and slapped it against his chest. "Sorry I asked. I'll just go back to my whorish ways now and stop bothering you."

Beau caught her arm. "Lily, stop. I didn't mean it that way."

"Yeah?" She pulled free, as if she couldn't stand his touch anymore, but then got right up in his face. "Then please explain to me what you actually meant. And be sure to use small words so I can understand."

Holding his hands up in surrender, he slowly backed up to the bookcase and latched it shut. "I meant I don't know if what I just saw down there means anything at all, but I have a strong feeling that it does. I sent a message to my team to look into it."

Her temper deflated enough for her to settle back on her heels, but she still crossed her arms defiantly. "Translate the message for me."

A decision tree formed in his mind, with so many options and possible scenarios, it'd take him a month to fully process each one—a month he didn't have. He was at the end of his allotted week, with a pissed-off Lily glaring at him and no doubt just waiting for the sun to rise so she could officially kick him out of her life and get back to hers. If Beau wanted to have a chance in hell of catching the informant and not lose Lily in the process, he'd have to trust her.

When had losing Lily become as important as confirming the identity of a traitor?

It hadn't, he realized. It wasn't *as* important. It was *more* important. For the first time in his adult life, Beau's loyalties were split and he wasn't quite sure how to handle it. What he knew without a doubt, however, was that he didn't want to see Lily walking out of his life.

And that decided it. "Pigeon is a term we use for possible suspects. Not confirmed, but a person of interest. There were two of them down there. Mister Menu is still on the premises. Broken wing. Not going anywhere. The other was a blond guy who paid his bill and left after Mister Menu went off with Amalia. Broken foot mean he's on the move, but we don't know where he's going. It means I want them to follow him."

Lily gaped. "You actually told me."

Beau let out the breath he hadn't realized he'd been holding. "Yeah. I told you."

"Thank you," she said.

"You're welcome."

Lily knew what it must have cost him to divulge his secret code. The fact that he trusted her enough to even share that much meant more to her than anything else he could have said or done. As before, Beau had once again unwittingly found the chink in her armor, only this time, instead of breaking it apart, he sealed it shut, made her strong again.

"So what happens now?" In the morning his week would be up, and now that he had not one but *two* possible suspects, he wouldn't want to waste time here with her anymore. Would he walk out without a backward glance? Would she have to see him with the other six every time they came into Miss Kiki's and pretend the last seven days had never happened?

"Now the real work starts." He checked his phone again, sent off another message, and Lily was half-convinced he'd already forgotten she was still in the room, when he sighed and tossed the phone onto her couch. "But first, come here."

Lily smiled. "Why don't you come here, instead?"

She let him stalk her around the couch and back into the bedroom; let him strip her bare and lay her out on the bed; let him worship her body with long, languorous strokes, and bit her tongue against the words desperately trying to claw their way up her throat.

I love you.

Don't leave me.

Those words still hovered on the tip of her tongue long after they'd fallen apart, spent, panting, their hands still clasped together. She fell asleep against his side, foolishly imagining this last week stretching forward into a lifetime of nights like this.

Lily had never slept more deeply, more peacefully than she did that night, only to wake the next morning to an empty space where Beau should have been.

Frowning, she sat up. Bathroom open and empty. Silence in the living room. No telltale sound of a boiling teapot in the kitchen. "Beau?"

No answer.

Terrified he'd left without saying goodbye, she bolted out of bed. "Beau, are you here?" She was about to open the bookcase and check the balcony, when she noticed the necklace lying on her coffee table next to a folded note.

Lily stared at that piece of paper, her knees going weak, her numb fingers clutching at the bookshelves for balance. Eventually, she forced herself to walk the five feet toward the table. That was as far as she got before her knees buckled and she sat down hard on the floor, still staring.

At last, she couldn't take it anymore and snatched up the note, clutching it in her fist a moment longer before she opened it. There, in the middle of that small, white rectangle, Beau's neat, small script spelled out what he couldn't tell her himself:

*Had to meet with my team and didn't want to wake you.
Back as soon as I can.*

Love, Beau

That's when Lily decided she might just have to kill the man.

CHAPTER 10

The bad news was that his team hadn't found who the blond pigeon answered to. They'd followed him to the west end slums, but lost him amid abandoned huts and piles of trash. He must have spotted one of them. Beau wasn't happy, but he kept his opinion to himself. For now, he could only hope that the pigeon would feel confident enough to have lost them and wouldn't bother alerting his boss.

The good news was that his other team had found who Mister Menu answered to. The information had put Beau into what his Network affectionately referred to as a tailspin.

Somehow, a threat the size of an elephant had managed to slip through the cracks and had sidled up to Queen Snow like a flea-bitten stray. Beau didn't even have time to blame himself—this lead was too big to be unsure about, which meant he'd need to get ironclad confirmation before presenting it to Snow, and for that, he couldn't rely on middlemen, messengers, or go-betweens. He'd need to lure out the main players and get them to meet face-to-face.

Snow's unscheduled board meeting would be starting in an hour. Would the "news" she had to share be enough to force their hand? Knowing what he did about the informant, Beau had no doubt it would. But to get the evidence he needed, he'd have to create a perfect, controlled opportunity for a covert meeting to take place. And for that, he'd need Lily's help.

He should have gone home to change before coming back, but hadn't wanted to waste an instant on vanity when there was so much work to be done. As a result, he walked back into Miss Kiki's through the front door, still wearing his Rebel Court uniform, which hadn't been washed in a couple of days. His shirt was undone and only half tucked into his pants, his cufflinks were gone, and his pants were crumpled like a cheap cleaning rag. He'd be embarrassed if he didn't have more important issues to think about.

Almost to the curtained-off hallway, Beau saw something out of the corner of his eye that made him backtrack to the fireplace. "Haig?" At least he thought it was Haig. The man looked like he'd just come back from a battlefield, complete with clothes far dirtier than Beau's, a beard, and a thousand-yard stare. Amazing that the bouncers hadn't turned him away from the door.

Roused by the sound of his voice, Haig frowned up at him. "Beau? What are you doing here?"

Beau rubbed the back of his neck self-consciously. This could get awkward. "Queen's orders."

Haig's eyebrows shot up. "The queen ordered you to get laid? Oh, man, that's embarrassing. I'm sorry it had to come to this."

Ever the fucking funny man. And Beau hated that he still rose to the bait, his face heating up bright red. "Will you shut up? That's not what this is about." It was merely a pleasant side effect.

"Should I congratulate you now or later?"

Beau's heretofore lack of sexual experience had never been a secret among the Rebel Seven, but out of respect, none of the others ever talked about it. Sadly, Haig didn't understand the meaning of the word *respect*, and though he never mentioned it in so many words when they were in public, he took great pleasure in tormenting Beau with insinuations, innuendos, and wagging eyebrows. If the man wasn't a brother, Beau would have punched his lights out by now. Multiple times, just to drive his point all the way home through Haig's thick skull.

Except this time, looking him over, Beau didn't have the heart. "Is something wrong? You look like hell."

Haig rubbed his stubbled chin and winced. "Yeah, I'm fine. Mission accomplished. All's well that ends well and all that shit."

"Doesn't sound like it ended all that well. You're about a month's worth of hair growth away from Graeme status."

Haig hissed. "Ouch, Beau. That was harsh."

"I just mean you look like you've been through a battle. What happened?"

Haig waved a careless hand. "Got into a bit of trouble with the Huntsman's daughter."

"Oh?" This was interesting. And there were so many ways that vague comment could be interpreted. He dropped into the seat next to Haig, leaned forward, and nodded for him to continue.

"It's nothing," Haig declared, scowling at the floor. "It's over. Back to life as usual."

"Right." Beau scoffed. That's why the consummate skirt chaser renowned throughout Kesteran for his utter inability to keep his dick in his pants was sulking—in a brothel—with all the girls sighing over him from afar. "So you won't be seeing the Huntress again?" He couldn't believe he'd just asked that question, but how else was he supposed to understand this? Haig *never* turned down anything with breasts and a pulse.

Haig frowned a little, stared off into space again, and Beau almost felt sorry for his friend.

"Well, I'm sure it's all for the best. You broke it off clean, right?" After a couple of seconds he realized Haig wouldn't answer, so he brushed it off. "Yeah, so take some time to get your head on straight, maybe have a drink, or an orgy, or whatever it is you like to do, and get over it. Snow's holding an unscheduled board meeting at the castle. I think it's gonna be big. She—"

Haig pushed to his feet. "Beau, I'll see you later," he said, already heading for the door with the purposeful strides of a man who finally had somewhere else he'd rather be.

Beau grinned. "You're welcome!"

Lily wasn't in her apartment and she hadn't left any notes about her schedule today. For all he knew, she'd have back-to-back appointments until tomorrow, and he couldn't wait that long to talk to her. Dropping his jerkin on the couch, he left the apartment and went in search of her.

Miss Kiki's was a maze of hallways leading to dead ends; grand, gilded doorways that opened onto cramped utility closets with strategically situated pails turned upside down; theater-like chambers with curtained stages; bedrooms that looked like they'd been copied from the castle's designs; and dungeons he didn't venture too far into. Everywhere he looked, he found discrete nooks and crannies that were just private enough to minimize interruptions, but still out in the open for anyone to see.

Beau shrugged. *To each their own, as long as all parties are willing.*

Thinking about what it'd be like to cozy up to Lily in one of those alcoves, Beau stopped paying attention to where he was going and almost ran into someone around the next corner.

"Whoa! Are you okay? Are you lost?"

Beau winced. Peter, one of the good old boys. "Yeah, sorry. Didn't mean to skulk. I'm looking for Lily. Have you seen her around?"

Peter was what Snow would have called "super pretty." He had a full head of long, silky hair and a wiry build. He moved with the fluid grace of a ballet dancer, and his face was so ridiculously symmetrical, it'd make classical artists weep. Slap some makeup and a dress on him, and he'd make one gorgeous woman. But paradoxically, he wasn't effeminate at all, and from what Beau had observed, his clientele was more female than male. "She's about to start an appointment."

"Oh." Shit.

Peter raised an eyebrow. "Was there anything you needed?"

"Uh… Nah, it can wait."

"Aw, come on now. It must be important if you came all the way back here, looking for her." Pretty Peter's pale blue eyes laughed at him, and he spoke a handful of words that couldn't possibly lead to anything good: "I've got an idea."

Once again, Lily was faced with the conundrum that was Mr. Jay. This time, he'd requested a heathen slave warrior, today played by Peter, servicing his high-class owner, Lily. It had taken her two hours to properly braid her hair and apply golden paint all over her arms and in strategic swirls on her torso and legs. She wore what amounted to a golden bib for a top, a translucent blue sheath tied around her hips for a skirt, and anklets with bells that jingled every time she moved.

She'd set the scene, entering a steam-filled bathing room with a hot tub built into the marble floor and colorful pillows scattered about. The set designer had also added a wine jug and a bowl of grapes, conveniently placed within Mr. Jay's reach. Everything was ready, Mr. Jay already squirming in his seat, all but whimpering when she ambled closer to take a grape. It was time to begin.

"Slave!"

The door opened behind her, admitting her partner. Chains clattered against the floor as he knelt. "My lady."

Lily froze. That was *not* Peter's voice. Steeling herself not to break character, she turned around and gawked. Thank goodness Mr. Jay couldn't see her face.

Kneeling before her, shoulders proudly back and head bowed in submission, was Beau Legeare, naked, except for a leather loincloth and chains cuffing his wrists and ankles. *What the hell is Beau doing in my scene?!*

Her answer stood just outside the door. Peter grinned at her, winked like the bastard he was, and closed the door, trapping her in a room with her client and her Rebel. If she broke the scene, Miss Kiki would have her head. If she broke it because of the man she'd been living with for the last week, her aunt would blow a gasket and turn her out. *No lovers, boyfriends, or husbands allowed.* Lily was so screwed.

Beau glanced up at her, must have seen her expression, and dropped his gaze again. "What is your will?"

Holy shit! *Get it together. Get it together.* Peter had dragged him into this; he must have explained the scene. And Beau was going along with it—for whatever crazy reason. This could work. She had to make this freaking work!

Taking a deep breath, she let it out slowly and put everything from her mind except her scene. "Tell me your name," she said.

"I'm—"

"You are no one. You are nothing. You have no name, unless I deign to give you one. Your life is mine, and you will obey my every command without question. Do you understand?"

Mr. Jay hissed, "*Yessss…*"

Beau must have heard him, but he still answered, "Yes, my lady."

"Stand up."

He did, still keeping his head down, but from beneath his lashes, he watched every step she took toward him. His hands fisted against his thighs, the loincloth tenting admirably.

Lily came toe-to-toe with him and whispered, "What are you doing here?" Then she turned around, presenting him with her back. "Take off my necklace, slave."

"As my lady wishes," he replied, then added in a whisper, "I had to talk to you."

"*Now?*"

"No! I wanted to wait, but then Peter happened."

"Well?" she said loudly. "What are you waiting for?"

"Yes, my lady." He reached up, his knuckles trailing a hot path up her spine to the necklace clasp that held her top in place. "By the way," Beau whispered at her ear, "you look absolutely stunning."

Lily couldn't prevent her smile if she tried.

He took his time undoing the clasp, but it finally came loose. She caught the top as it slid down her front, and tossed it aside. "Now the skirt. And don't you dare tear it!"

"Yes, my lady." His hands smoothed down her sides to the knot at her hip. He pulled it loose, careful not to damage the delicate fabric.

Mr. Jay started panting as the vibrator in his seat cranked up a notch. Lily sighed. He wouldn't last another five minutes.

But Beau would. When he pulled the skirt from her, she turned around again to face him and show off her ass to Mr. Jay. "Look at you," she sneered. "Filthy, like the animal you are. Do you think I'll let you touch me with those disgusting, dirty hands?"

"No, my lady. I'm sorry, my lady."

"Get in the bath and kneel," she ordered.

"Yes, my lady." He made his way over, somehow managing to look proud and strong, even as the chain stretching between his ankles kept his steps pathetically short. He struggled going down the two stairs into the water. When he knelt, the surface barely came up to his mid-thigh. The tub was more for show than actual bathing, good for getting a body wet, but not deep enough to fully submerge, and they kept the water crystal clear so no one ever missed a thing.

"Take off your clothes." Pathetic as they were.

He jerkily complied, but he flushed with embarrassment to be naked in front of someone else. She'd have to break him of that in the future, but for now, it helped make his character more believable. Lily touched a hand to her collarbone, slid it down to her breast. "Now bathe."

Beau leaned forward, scooped some water up, and splashed his face. He repeated this three more times, splashing handfuls of water over his chest, shoulders, and back. Then he sat back on his heels, his cock bobbing just above the surface, and waited for more instructions. As the proud warrior enduring humiliation, he stared straight ahead, as if too affronted to keep his gaze on the floor any longer.

"More," she ordered, teasing her own nipple.

Beau dipped his hand into the bowl of "soap" beside him, which was really just oil, and began rubbing it on his chest and stomach. He flexed for her, too, displaying wiry muscles in his biceps and a rigid set of abs. The oil had a unique warming quality that stimulated the skin. He noticed, too, his gaze flickering to her briefly, before he faced forward again.

"More, slave! Wash everywhere."

Mr. Jay whimpered, seconds away from blowing his load.

Beau dipped his hand into the bowl again and brought it to his torso, oiling up his abs some more then burnishing his delicious, hard cock with a couple of hygienic strokes before moving on to his thighs.

Mr. Jay ate it up, especially when Lily smoothed a hand between her legs, but she wasn't having it. "Did I tell you to stop, slave?"

"No, my lady."

"Then get back to work. I want that cock nice and clean, you hear?"

Beau turned his head to look right at her. "Yes, my lady." Dark eyes burning with need, he kept his gaze on her and nothing else as he took his cock in hand and began to stroke.

Lily couldn't have imagined a more arousing setup. She watched him work his flesh, matched his rhythm with her own fingers between her legs. "Faster," she commanded, but her voice was too breathy and completely lacking authority. She was getting caught up in her own pleasure, watching him masturbate to the sight of her getting herself off.

Sensing weakness, Beau smirked a little. "As my lady commands." He picked up speed and so did she, finger-fucking herself hard and fast, the client completely forgotten as she and Beau stared at each other. She came with a sharp cry, catching herself against the wine table. Beau exhaled on a hard burst of air, kept pumping that hand until she said, "Stop. Stop." With one last stroke, he did, but didn't let go.

Mr. Jay wasn't as obedient. He was already wailing his orgasm, but Lily didn't care. She got on her hands and knees and crawled over to the side of the tub where the floor sloped dramatically toward the client seating. "Are you clean yet, slave?"

Bereft of words, Beau nodded.

"Are you sure?"

"Yes, my lady," he said, his voice so hoarse it was almost a growl.

"Then I guess it's my turn." With her ass against the edge of the pool, she lay back, downhill, and braced her feet on either side, spreading her knees wide. "You know what to do."

Beau dipped both hands in the bowl, got them nice and slick before he knee-walked toward her. He started at her belly, massaging the warm oil into her skin with masterful dexterity. Up her torso, one hand briefly curled around her throat, his chains chilling her, making her nipples bead harder. Down over her breasts, lingering, teasing, then lower over her side to her ass, jerking her closer in a very un-slave-like move that made her gasp.

"Watch yourself, slave."

"I'd rather watch you, my lady," he replied, continuing his massage over her legs and loins.

"Impertinent."

"Always, my lady." He retrieved the bowl, tipped it over her, drizzling oil right over her pussy. The tingling intensified every touch as he rubbed her thoroughly from her clit down to her pussy and inside. Her hips curled up, and he pressed them down once more with his free hand. "Does my lady approve?"

In some far corner of her mind not currently overstimulated by Beau's master fingering technique, Lily heard Mr. Jay moving around. His chair was still vibrating; he was watching with rapt attention, and knowing that she had two men entranced with nothing but her body made her feel like, for these two hours at least, she was the most amazing thing in the world.

But she'd be lying if she said Beau being one of them wasn't the main reason for her euphoric state.

"My lady is quiet. Shall I stop?"

"No! Don't stop. Don't…"

He set back in, bringing her to the very edge, then pulling back. Again and again. "Gods!" A week into his sexual awakening and he'd already surpassed every pro she'd ever partnered with. "I want your cock, slave. Give it to me. Now!"

"Yes, my lady. He crawled over her, holding himself up on his hands, letting her reach down to guide him into place. She stroked him a few times first before she let him slide in. After that, she couldn't speak a word, couldn't do anything except hold on as he drove into her, slick, hard, and hot.

He fucked her into an orgasm so powerful her eyes rolled back and her entire body quivered. It had barely faded when Beau pushed up to kneel so he could finger her clit in time with his thrusts, sending her over again, making her scream. Her body became putty in his hands. He pulled out and turned her over onto her stomach with her legs spread wide. More oil poured onto her back, her ass. He circled his thumb around her anus, pressed against it just enough to let her feel him as he fed his cock back into her pussy.

She didn't have the strength to tell him what she wanted, but she didn't need to. Beau seemed to know her body's needs better than Lily herself. When she arched back to him, he pushed his thumb into her ass to the first knuckle. Lily came apart again, shaking, clawing at the marble floor, torn between asking for more and begging for him to stop.

"Is my lady satisfied?" She could tell from his voice that he was close, and rallied herself enough for one more order, for Mr. Jay's benefit.

"You will not come inside me, slave."

"Yes, my lady," he rasped. Three more thrusts hard enough to jar her across the floor, and he pulled out with a hoarse shout.

She felt his cum on her back and sighed. "Now you'll have to clean me again."

CHAPTER 11

A re you sure?"

At this juncture, Beau had no other choice. Right after Lily's appointment, they'd rushed back to her apartment and Beau had found sixteen messages on his phone. His team had identified the blond pigeon: Arnaud Emmanuel Kincade. Part-time pickpocket, full-time hustler, and one smartass bastard. He had them chasing their own tails, which only confirmed Beau's suspicion that he was on to them.

After giving them all the slip, Kincade had sauntered right back into Miss Kiki's like he owned the place. He'd sat in the middle of the common room, with a shit-eating grin on his face, his feet up on the table, a jug of ale in hand, and Amalia toying with his open shirt.

Amalia again. Mister Menu's girl of choice the night before. Was she in on this? He couldn't be sure without doing more digging, and he couldn't do that without blowing his cover. Which was why, against Lily's many protests, they now stood in front of her aunt's office, about to break every one of Beau's cardinal rules.

"Are you *really* sure?" she asked again.

He nodded, the same way he had in her apartment, and in the secret stairwell leading down from it, and in the hallway, and just outside the kitchen, after she'd come back out of it with a handful of chocolate meringues.

Lily shook her head. "I don't like this."

"Believe me, neither do I."

Lily sighed, adjusting the modest-for-her backless dress she'd put on for this meeting. "Okay then, let's go say hi to Auntie Dragon." She knocked hard, then stepped back to stand beside him while they waited.

Miss Kiki herself opened the door, dressed in a bright red pencil skirt suit, her hair pulled back into a tight bun, a pearl necklace adorning her pale throat, and her thick-rimmed glasses perched on the very tip of her nose. She looked surprised to see them.

Smiling brightly, Lily said, "Hi, Aunt! You got a minute for your favorite niece?"

Miss Kiki's eyes narrowed at her niece, then her shrewd gaze slid over to Beau. He nodded in greeting but didn't say a word. Miss Kiki's mouth twisted in disapproval, then, without looking away from him, she stepped back. "You two better come in."

Beau waved Lily in first and followed right after her. Somehow, the office didn't look like he'd pictured it, but it fit the woman to a T. Comfortable enough to lull a person into a sense of complacency, with just enough formality to keep them off balance.

Miss Kiki seated herself in an armchair, Lily took a spot on the couch, which left Beau with the love seat opposite her to form a U among the three of them. A tense silence choked off any available air while Miss Kiki looked from Beau to Lily, waiting for one of them to speak. Except Beau hadn't told Lily any details yet, so she couldn't say anything, and Beau felt too much like a new boyfriend being introduced to his girl's guardian to think up any clever intros.

Finally, Miss Kiki sat back and opened the fancy little box on the mini-table next to her, taking out a piece of chocolate. "I'm going to assume that *this* is the mysterious person living in your apartment." The lilt at the end of that sentence made it a question.

"Yes, Aunt," Lily replied.

"And the 'new guy' Mr. Jay just requested for all future appointments?"

Who?

Lily blushed and wouldn't look at him. "Yes, Aunt." She sat ramrod straight at the edge of the couch, reminding him of the little girl she'd been when they'd first met. Except even back then she'd never been so polite and demure. She was making an effort for his sake, to appease her aunt, but Beau hated that she did; hated that she felt she had to, because it was clearly making her miserable.

"And I assume this sudden visit is not for Beau to negotiate a contract with me."

Lily looked to him, mouth open to speak, but no words came out. "I approached Miss Maverick for assistance in a delicate matter concerning the crown," he said, deciding to play this as safe as possible—for Lily's sake.

"I see," Miss Kiki said.

Beau couldn't read the woman at all. "We have a situation, possibly involving one of your employees. I haven't been able to confirm yet whether she's directly involved, or being used as a pawn, but—"

"But you have your suspicions, which I would be a fool to ignore." Miss Kiki smiled a little, set her uneaten chocolate aside, and lightly clasped her hands together in her lap. Beau had never felt more threatened before in his entire life. "Neither of us got to where we are today by being stupid, Beau. You have my attention and, as always, my loyalty. Give me a name, and I'll take care of it."

Lily opened her mouth to reply, but Beau cut her off. "Actually, that's not why we're here." As quickly as he could, he outlined his mission, Lily's involvement, and what he needed to do now.

"So this man you had followed is sitting in my establishment right now."

"Yes, ma'am."

"He came right back to the scene of the crime, to the same woman? Why would he do that?"

"Because he's overconfident. He's lost my people twice now, and knows we don't have anything on him, or whoever he works for. He came back to rub it in our faces, to flaunt his own prowess."

"You sound certain."

"I am. I know his kind. I've *been* his kind before the war. I understand how he thinks, because I've thought the same until I joined up with the Rebels. He feels untouchable, because he has no ties to anyone—no family, no friends, or lovers. There's no one we can use against him, so he has absolutely nothing to lose."

He felt Lily staring at him and looked across the coffee table to find her eyes shimmering with tears. Beau felt heat rising in his cheeks again and frowned at her in silent question. But Lily shook her head and looked away, covertly wiping her nose.

"I see," Miss Kiki replied. She studied him for a moment before asking, "So what do you need from me?"

"All we have right now are suspicions. I can't move on those, and neither can Queen Snow; we need solid proof. We need to catch this guy in the act, with plenty of witnesses willing to testify if necessary."

"You're asking me to put my people in a position to rat out their most loyal clients. Would you do the same with your people?"

There was no rancor in her tone; she was still the calm, collected—*cold*—matron who'd opened the door ten minutes ago. Damn, if Snow could get this woman on her board, Valefort would never want for anything. "No, ma'am, I would never ask that of you, your employees, or mine. If all goes as planned, there will be plenty of other witnesses around who'll have nothing to lose by testifying. All I'm asking for is the opportunity."

Another contemplative silence.

"Aunt, we can do this," Lily said, leaning forward as if she could influence her aunt's decision with the force of her will alone. "We already have the perfect setup—"

"Don't speak for me, girl. You haven't earned the right." Then, in a softer tone, Miss Kiki added, "*Yet.*" She pushed to her feet and glided over to a massive bookcase. Selecting a thick binder from among dozens, she brought it back to her seat and flipped through the pages inside. "Supreme Judge Lester Chang is already on the list of invitees for the Masquerade. The invitations were sent out this morning. What more would you like me to do?"

Supreme Judge Lester Chang. The man in charge of passing final judgment on corporate court cases worth millions of ducats in legal fees alone. The former member of Zorana's advisory council who'd earned his current high position by blowing the whistle on Zorana's corrupt dealings and securing himself not only Snow White's good will, but also her trust. Where the other members of Zorana's court remained under strict watch, a few had proven themselves loyal to the new regime. Until last night, Beau had considered Chang to be one of them.

"If he asks, grant him a special invite for an additional guest." From what Lily had told him about the Masquerade, Miss Kiki was inundated with special invite requests every year, but they were always from the people who *hadn't* gotten an invite themselves. To request one for someone else would be an excellent way for Chang to implicate himself.

It was definitely a long shot, but what the hell? Maybe the lure would prove too tasty to resist and they'd catch Chang *and* his associate without ever needing to resort to Plan A. Strategies were built around weak spots, points of uncertainty that ultimately created opportunities for people like Beau.

"And if he doesn't?"

"We'll have to assume that whoever he's feeding information to is already invited, as well."

"Those are some very big assumptions you're operating under," Miss Kiki noted, closing the binder in her lap. "The biggest of which is that these men will actually meet here for the Masquerade at all, let alone for the purpose of insider trading."

Beau winced. "You're right. For all I know, we've already blown our chance by following the two messengers and they've changed their mode of operation completely. But I'm not ready to close the book on this until I am absolutely *sure*. This is too big to allow for any loose ends." He had to believe the news Snow delivered would force their hand and make them slip up.

Chang was extremely high profile—he and anyone he met with would stand out anywhere, except here, during the Masquerade.

"What's your contingency plan if you fail to obtain your evidence?"

"Queen Snow has put events into motion that should eventually flush out the judge's associates. But this is the best chance we'll ever get to implicate the judge himself. We need to take it. Will you help us?"

Miss Kiki went back to the bookcase and replaced the binder, then straightened a few others before returning to her seat. "I'd like to speak to my niece for a moment in private, if you don't mind."

Beau frowned. "She's not involved—"

"Let me be the judge of that. If you'd please wait in the meeting room through that door there, I promise I won't keep either of you long."

Beau looked to Lily who shrugged, wide-eyed. "All right," he relented. "I'll be right outside." But he didn't like it. Not at all.

Lily expected a thorough browbeating, or at least a stern lecture to come from Aunt Tabitha as soon as the door closed after Beau. Instead, her aunt sat back down, quietly studying Lily with the same look of unruffled serenity she'd worn all through their meeting so far.

And Lily began to get really nervous. "Aunt—"

"Do you know what you're doing, girl?"

"I'm making a small payment on the debt we'll all owe for the rest of our lives. I thought you'd be on board with this without question."

"I'm not talking about Beau's mission, Lily, I'm talking about Beau."

Wary of this sudden change of direction, Lily frowned. "What about Beau?"

Tabitha crossed her legs at the ankles and leaned forward. "Let me ask you something. Please forgive the banality, but where do you see yourself in ten years?"

"Uh…"

"Think about it for a minute. I know how much you love working here, but this can't be all you've ever aspired to, spending your life being used by anyone who can pay, giving half of your profits over to the House. You're so much smarter than that, Lily."

"What are you saying?" She really hoped it wasn't what she thought, but something told her it was.

"If it'd been any other man in the world, I wouldn't have batted an eye. But don't think I somehow missed that massive torch you've been carrying for that boy ever since you saw him ten years ago. You used to draw his name in hearts on your mirror—wasting a lot of very expensive lipstick in the process, I might add."

"What's your point?"

"My point is, what if this is your one chance to make a relationship with him work? What if you won't ever get another?"

"And all I have to do to make it happen is give up everything I have and everything I've ever been. Is that it?"

Never one to tolerate attitude from any of her employees, Aunt Tabitha straightened in her seat, her no-nonsense resting bitch face firmly in place. "Take it as you will. It's your life, your choice. You've made quite a name for yourself here, Lily, but believe me when I say it won't last. No matter how much you want it to. The spirit may be willing, but the body gets old, tired. You'll wake up one day and find that your oldest clients are going to the younger girls. You'll go to your appointments already bored, wishing you could have stayed home and watched TV. You'll want someone of your own eventually, and men of Beau's caliber don't wait forever."

"Sage words of wisdom from one whore to another," Lily retorted. "But then, I don't see you slowing down, settling in with your honey for the night."

Aunt Tabitha smiled, her eyes gleaming with a vicious spark Lily had never seen before. "But you don't see me taking orders from anyone, either, do you?"

Lily gulped. No, she did not. In Valefort's thriving sex industry, Miss Kiki was a self-made legend. She'd rebuilt her house from its own ashes, made it bigger, better—a house without equal. In their world, Miss Kiki's was the capital of sex, and the proud proprietor was its queen.

"Is this your way of giving me a chance to quit before you fire me?"

Aunt Tabitha sighed. "This is my way of telling you I love you. I want you to be happy, and if being part of *my* house was it, I'd let you stay as long as your heart desired. But we both know it's not; you're only here because it's safe. As long as you have me to fall back on, you don't have to take any risks, and I won't have you rotting away here when you could be doing so much more on your own."

Lily snorted. "Right, yeah. Makes sense. I'll just go out there and start my own house, why don't I?"

The caustic retort she'd expected never came.

"Maybe I'll take over one of those fancy mansions across town that Zorana's court abandoned. Wouldn't that be a hoot? A brothel in some uptight prick's home sweet home."

Aunt Tabitha's lips twitched just a little. Why wasn't she bashing the idea? Why wasn't she setting down new rules and adding non-compete clauses to her contract?

Getting desperate for any kind of contradiction, Lily grasped at straws. "I'll call it Hothouse Flowers and every girl will be named after a different flower! You like that? I'll take all of my clients away from Miss Kiki's and have an annual Christmas bash open to everyone for an insanely exorbitant price, and nothing will be off-limits. I'll build up a house to end all houses, even yours, and you'll rue this day and hate yourself for ever putting the idea in my head!"

Her aunt raised an eyebrow and smiled. "Now you're thinking, girl." She pushed to her feet and went to let Beau back in, as mellow as you please, as if she hadn't just sent Lily into a panic attack.

Her own house? What was she thinking?

Of course, she had the money saved up, and her client list was substantial and loyal to a fault. She even had friends among the girls who'd happily follow her to get out from Miss Kiki's thumb and her 50% commission rate. But that wasn't the point! They were supposed to be working on Beau's secret mission, not Lily's retirement plan.

Holy shit! Do I want to retire? She'd never thought that far ahead, figuring she'd do this until she became old and repugnant and then jump off a bridge or whatever. Who cared? That was still decades away, and her Hothouse money could just as easily be a Cosmetic Enhancement fund.

When the hell did it become "Hothouse money," for fuck's sake?!

Lily raked her hair back, curled her fists around it, and tugged. This was not happening. She was never leaving Miss Kiki's and that was that. She did not care about the massive amount of money a little competition could bring them both. Or about how freaking good "Madame Lily" sounded in her head. She was definitely not going to be making any plans for interior decor, or landscaping—but obviously there would be plush carpeting and lots of flower motifs throughout, water features, and an underground cellar for a rough-play dungeon.

Nope, none of that would ever happen. Because her ass was staying right here, and Beau would just have to deal with that!

"What?" Lily demanded when they stared at her. "I didn't say anything."

"Yeah, we know. We're waiting for you to answer."

"Oh. What was the question again?"

"Do you think the dryad glen can accommodate one more male in the cast?" Aunt Tabitha said, fighting hard not to let that twitchy-lip stretch into an outright smile. Conniving old bitch.

"Why would we need another male?"

"Beau will need to be there to gather his evidence."

"I offered to use the concealment charm—"

"There'll be too many people for that; they'll slam into him left and right. So he just volunteered to get into costume and join in." And there went her eyebrows, shooting up toward her hairline. If she were a normal person, she'd be jumping up and down, cheering, "Get him, girl! Lock that stallion up before he gets away!"

The poor man might not have any idea what he'd just done, but Lily did.

He'd earned Miss Kiki's normally unobtainable stamp of approval. Gods save him…

Lily shook her head to recover her power of speech. "Uh, I suppose we could add one more. But that'll trap you in the room for the night."

She expected to see him melt through the floor in relief, but instead Beau frowned in thought, then made a face. "She's right. I'll need freedom to move about; to steer him where I need him to go, and keep an eye on him the entire time, and somehow keep my identity secret." Not exactly a walk in the park. He was already doing that zoning-out thing he did when calculating all probabilities.

"Right," Lily said to get his attention back to the present moment.

"Can't do any of that as one of the entertainers."

"So you'll have to attend as a guest yourself," Aunt Tabitha added in delight. "It's a masquerade, after all." One which none of the Rebels had ever attended before. For Beau to be the first would be an unimaginable conquest for her—something Tabitha was well aware of, if the cat-that-ate-the-canary look on her face was any indication. "Do you have suitable attire for the occasion? If not, I can offer you the services of my seamstress."

Beau gave a gallant bow. "I would be most grateful for your assistance, Madam."

Yeah, you say that now…

CHAPTER 12

On Friday morning, Beau woke up on the floor of Lily's balcony. He groaned, joints cracking as he got up and stretched. The common room downstairs was almost empty, cleaning crews wiping up spilled drinks and straightening the furniture—with passed-out patrons still on them. The grandfather clock read ten in the morning, but it was still a bit dark outside. Heavy storm clouds obscured the sky, thunder already rumbling in the distance. This one would be huge.

Beau reached for his phone, only to remember he'd left it on the living room table the night before. He should go check it. But Lily didn't have any appointments today, which meant she'd probably be in there, leafing through her magazine, pretending she wasn't freaking out over whatever her aunt had told her yesterday after sending him out of the room. She wouldn't tell him what it was, either.

This entire mission had just spiraled so far out of his control, he was grasping at frayed threads to get *something*. Beau's ratio of on-duty-to-in-bed time had somehow gotten skewed to hell and back, his team had blown their covers, he'd been forced to announce his presence and purpose to the business proprietor, and the biggest secret he'd ended up keeping was that despite ten years of telling himself he'd blown his childhood crush on Lily far out of proportion, Beau was still hopelessly in love with her.

She'd probably laugh in his face if she knew.

And then there was the impending orgy. Odds of Chang showing up: one-to-one. Odds of him doing anything other than participating in the most prestigious fuckfest in Kesteran: one hundred and fifty thousand-to-one. Beau had a better chance of getting struck by lightning while bending over to pick up a Zorana-era copper ducat. For all intents and purposes, this mission was a bust, and the orgy would only hammer the final nail in the coffin. If it had been any other assignment, he'd have delegated it to an underling and pursued other, more promising leads long before now.

Gods, he'd fucked this up so much. Worse, now he'd have to report it to Snow. *Your Majesty, I regret to inform you that I was unable to keep my dick in my pants for even a day—an hour!—and now our best chance to uncover the informant is to risk exposing my identity as your spymaster in front of a hundred people fucking their brains out.*

That would go over well…

Wishing he'd never agreed to this insanity in the first place, Beau went back inside.

"Morning," Lily greeted without looking up from the open magazines spread out on the coffee table in front of her. She tore out a page from one of them, put it on one of the stacks on the floor. "Breakfast is on the table."

Beau nodded in thanks, but bypassed the meal in favor of a hot shower. He used Lily's towel to dry off, her razor to shave, her toothbrush to brush his teeth. He'd been doing that since day one, and Lily hadn't complained a single time. Now, suddenly he felt like the worst kind of parasite.

His clothes needed washing again. He tossed them down the laundry chute—something else he'd gotten far too comfortable with—and came out of the bathroom with just a towel wrapped around his hips. For the first time since he'd started living off Lily, her bed was perfectly made, and a stack of clothes sat at the foot.

"Aunt Tabitha sent up clothes for you," Lily called from the living room. "She said we have a standard to uphold here and it doesn't include desecrating the Rebel Court uniform with a week's worth of sweat and BO."

Beau cringed.

"You don't smell, Beau," she added dryly. "She's just being helpful. In her own, insulting way."

Marginally mollified, he dressed, and padded barefoot back to the dining table and the breakfast that had gotten cold already. He ate quickly, as always, washed all the dishes, and put the tray back in the dumbwaiter.

The apartment seemed cold. In the middle of summer, it wasn't chilly, exactly, but with the storm hovering and a cool cross-breeze blowing through, it felt as if it *should* be cold. Beau lit a small blaze in the fireplace, instantly comforted by its welcoming light and warmth.

He liked the sound of crackling wood, the scent of clean smoke perfuming the air. It always made him think of the campfires the Rebels had spent their evenings around. Sometimes there'd been game roasting over the flame, other times they'd gone hungry, but always they'd filled the silent nights with friendly banter and for a few hours at least they'd forgotten everything that'd happened that day and everything that awaited them come sunrise.

Today, that peace lasted all of fifteen seconds. The sound of tearing paper ripped it to shreds and reminded him where he was, with whom, and why. His cold breakfast sitting heavy in his gut, Beau asked. "Should we discuss payment?"

"No," Lily answered.

"Our arrangement was for a week. My bill is two days past due."

"Did you *see* a bill?"

"Well… No."

"Then shut up about it."

"Yeah, but—"

She slammed down a stack of magazines, startling him into looking at her where she glared at him over the back of the couch. "Why are you pushing this?"

Beau backpedaled quickly. "I'm sorry. I didn't mean anything by it. I just didn't want you to think that… I'm not presuming… We had an agreement, and I just want to honor it, that's all."

"So you think I'm letting you stay here all this time because of money?"

Danger! Trick question! "Aren't you?"

She flushed as he'd never seen her do before. Her gaze flicked sideways and back to him. "I—"

A loud knock at her front door cut off whatever she'd been about to say. She sighed, almost in relief, and went to answer it.

It didn't even occur to Beau that he might want to hide before Lily ushered a small, robust woman in a blue pantsuit into the living room. "Miss Kiki sent me to get your measurements for the costumes," the woman explained to him with a bright smile. "And may I just say, it's an honor to meet you, sir."

Shocked, Beau could only stare.

"Marcy's super discrete," Lily assured him, already taking off her clothes. "It's all right, Beau."

Too late now, anyway. He'd made his bed for the Masquerade, now he had to lie in it. Flushing beet red, Beau shrugged out of his T-shirt and sweatpants, folded them neatly on the couch, and faced the giggling Marcy with her measuring tape.

Gods, this could not possibly get any worse.

Marcy grinned at him, flicking her finger to indicate his underwear shorts. "We take our work very seriously around here, Mr. Legeare. I'll need to measure *all* of you."

And wrong again.

Lily saw the terror on Beau's face and burst out laughing, which didn't help the situation at all. But how was she supposed to keep a straight face when the poor guy looked like he'd rather jump out of the third-story window than let Marcy near him with her measuring tape?

And naturally the mischievous Marcy didn't tell him she was kidding so, of course, the kind-hearted Beau reluctantly dropped his shorts, which just made Lily laugh harder. Gods, she loved that adorable man. It scared the hell out of her, but she decided not to think about it for the moment.

Enjoy him while you can, but don't expect Happily Ever After.

No matter what Aunt Tabitha said, men like Beau didn't settle down with women like Lily. He might stick around for a while after this mission was through, might even tell himself he was okay with her "fucking strangers out of their money," but eventually he'd realize this life wasn't for him. He'd get territorial and jealous; he'd resent her for sharing herself with others, maybe even ask her to stop, and that would be the end.

Because as much as Lily loved having Beau here with her, she loved her job, too, and she wasn't ready to give it up. At least not any time soon. Better to end things on a high note. She wanted to have something beautiful to remember of her time with Beau—amazing sex, falling asleep cuddled up against him on the couch, sharing meals at her dining table. No regrets. No bitter fights, accusations, or resentment.

She wanted him to think of her fondly, too. She wanted to be the reason he looked back on his past and smiled when he was bouncing little kidlets on his knees while his proper, respectable wife read them fairy tales in front of the fireplace. Beau deserved that.

"Why are you looking at me like that?" Beau asked, scowling at Lily as Marcy took proper measurements for his costume.

Because once this is over, I'll have to find a way to say goodbye, and I don't think I can. Lily shrugged. "No reason." But she didn't look away, and something in his expression changed. Had he guessed at her thoughts?

"There! All done," Marcy pronounced. "You can get dressed now, handsome."

He couldn't dive for his clothes fast enough.

"Now it's your turn, missy."

"Yes, ma'am." Lily obediently straightened her spine, sucked in her stomach, and spread her arms. She was grateful Beau had lit a fire. It wasn't cold, exactly, but standing there naked except for a pair of silk panties, she still got goose bumps, especially as she watched Beau put his clothes back on.

Marcy looped the measuring tape around Lily's waist and poked her in the side. She knew all of Lily's tricks. Lily relaxed her abs, and Marcy scowled. "You've been stealing chocolate meringues again, haven't you?"

"Can I help it? They're just so good!"

"You know your aunt has rules about this. You're already at the upper limit. One more meringue and I'll have to report you."

"Woman, do *not* give her a complex," Beau growled.

Marcy glanced back at him, then gaped at Lily.

"What the customer wants, the customer gets," Lily said with a smug grin. Take that, stupid-ass weight rules. As if fucking a stick figure was in any way enjoyable.

Marcy rushed through the rest of her measurements, took some notes, and then left in a hurry, muttering something about first fittings tomorrow afternoon. Not like the seamstress had to spend much time on the bare-minimum costumes required for the orgy, since most of it would be water-resistant makeup, but Beau would be getting formalwear, custom designed and sewn together by Marcy's own hand—something she'd no doubt brag about for the rest of her life—so she was making them a priority.

"For the record," Beau said after Marcy left, "I like you exactly the way you are."

"Oh, yeah? Prove it."

And, to her delight, he did. Thoroughly.

It was the perfect afternoon, and the perfect evening when the storm finally broke, shrouding them in booming thunder and the roar of pouring rain. They lay in bed together, touching constantly, with affection rather than desire, and Lily was so content she wanted to purr.

Until Beau's phone went on the fritz with messages buzzing and ringing in one after the other. He left the bed, read through the missives, cursed, and reached for his clothes.

"Something wrong?"

"The team I put on Kincade was attacked. Three men down, one severely injured. I don't know what happened, but it sounds like they might have been ambushed."

Oh, shit. "Should you be going after them now? Won't that blow your cover?"

"I'm not going after them. They're at the hospital and have a team of healers looking out for them. I need to check in with the team I put on Chang, make sure they're being safe." He stuffed his feet into his boots, then came back to her and kissed her hard. "Keep the bed warm for me, love. I'll be back as soon as I can."

Then he was out the door, leaving Lily to stress all by herself. He hadn't even taken an umbrella. The man would get soaked through and probably end up in that damn hospital right alongside his men. And what if he got run over? What if he fell into the river and drowned? What if there was another ambush waiting for him?

Gods, what the hell is wrong with you? This wasn't like her. Lily didn't fret; she acted.

She got out of bed and put on her fluffy robe and slippers. Time to prove she wasn't just a borderline chubby body with a pretty face.

Picking up the house phone, she dialed an extension and waited for it to be picked up. "Hey girl! You busy tonight?"

"I was gonna be," Kendra replied. "My client cancelled because of the weather. Weak-willed bastard."

"Pajama party?"

"Oooh, will you have the good hot chocolate and marshmallows?"

"You know it! I might even order up a cheese fondue."

"Twist my arm, why dontcha. I'm there."

"Excellent! I'll call Harley and Benna. You get Amalia, Lacie, and Tess."

"Deal." *Click.*

She smiled. The best way to get those girls to talk was over decadent food and wine. Lots and lots of wine. She put away all of her magazines, stashed her "idea pages" into her storage chest so she wouldn't lose them, hid any evidence that a man had been staying with her, and set the coffee table with a raggedy old tablecloth and lots of napkins. With a few clicks, she ordered up the meal service, then she ran back into her bedroom to change into sweatpants and a flannel shirt.

The doorbell rang.

One last look around: everything in order. Lily rubbed her hands together and went to open the door. She settled her friends in and started pouring the wine, and kept pouring throughout the night, laughing with them, sharing food, but keeping her own glass half-full and untouched.

They gossiped about the men on staff, giggled over Aunt Tabitha's dictatorial rules, sighed over the Masquerade, and around midnight finally loosened up enough to talk clients. Lily poured more wine, brought out more treats, then quietly sat back to listen.

None of them paid much attention to her; they were having too much fun at their clients' expense and were too drunk to care that they probably shouldn't be sharing so much embarrassing information about them.

But it wasn't until Kendra brought up Mr. Jay's lack of stamina, that Amalia finally joined in with a few stories of her own, giggling like a ditz at a client who couldn't get off unless she repeated the ridiculous poems he wrote for her that never made sense. She didn't mind, though. It helped her with another client who couldn't get it up unless she spoke in rhymes. Instead of making up new ones on the spot, she just used the ones she got from Mr. Bad Poet, and he always appreciated it so much, he tipped her triple—which, of course, she never reported to her boss.

Lily took a sip of wine to hide her surprise. She'd never realized how resentful the girl was of everything she had going for her. The longer Amalia spoke, the more it bled through into her words, until her bitterness silenced all the laughter in the room and careless grins turned awkward before falling away completely. Amalia didn't notice.

Kendra cast a worried glance at Lily, silently communicating to her that someone should stop the madness before it cost Amalia her job and her home. Like Lily, most of the other girls lived at Miss Kiki's because it made things easier for them. Most, however, also had a separate apartment somewhere in the city for when they needed to get away from it all. Lily didn't have one, and she knew for a fact Amalia didn't, either—a fact the girl confirmed when she drunkenly admitted to making unsanctioned house calls to her high-end clientele on her days off so she'd have somewhere else to sleep.

Kendra gaped, then mouthed to Lily, *What the fuck?!*

Still, Amalia had to hammer in that last nail. "You know, we could all be making *sooo much more* if we went out on our own. Like, you know, for private parties, 'n stuff. Do you know how much those rich assholes pay for that shit? Like, I got this referral from Judge Chang once, gave me a sealed letter of reference 'n everything. Did a li'l show, a li'l poke, three hours tops. Easiest ten grand I ever made. And it was all mine." She giggled. "*Ten grand!* Can you imagine? Best I can get here is eight hundred, and half of that goes into someone else's pocket."

"Hey, all," Kendra said, taking Amalia's wine glass away from her as she was trying to refill it from an empty bottle. "I think it's time we call it a night. What do you say?"

The rest of them quickly hummed in agreement, picking themselves up off the floor. A couple had to be helped along, but they all thanked Lily as they filed out the door. Kendra, holding up Amalia, was the last one out. "I'll talk to the others, try to keep this under wraps. Miss Kiki hears about this shit, she's gonna flip the fuck out on this stupid bitch." Understatement of the century. When it came to her money, Aunt Tabitha did not fuck around. Breaching their exclusivity contracts made the girls liable for enormous damages, including one hundred percent of whatever they'd made on the side. "You won't tell her, will you?"

"Of course not!" Lily assured her. "I would never betray a confidence. You know that." Besides, she wasn't so much worried about Amalia's income as the shit she'd done to earn it.

Kendra smiled. "You're a doll. I'll see you tomorrow. *Mwah.*"

Lily closed the door. "Yeah. See you tomorrow."

CHAPTER 13

On Saturday, Beau spent the morning on his phone, so Lily left him to it and made some covert inquiries of her own. Under the guise of setting up her appointments for the coming week, she asked the housekeeper for a room schedule, then requested surveillance kits from the security team and snuck out to set them up in every room Amalia had reserved leading up to the Masquerade.

Miss Kiki's had a no-questions-asked policy about recording client sessions. While surveillance kits were sometimes used for clients who wanted an incredibly expensive memento in the form of amateur videos, any of the employees could request a kit for high-risk clients for safety reasons, as well. No questions asked, unless there was an incident.

Feeling like a master spy after accomplishing her task, Lily skipped back up to her apartment and ordered a fancy three-course lunch to celebrate. Beau didn't notice her setting the table, but he did notice when she put on music in the living room, then danced her way back across to light the little candle in the middle of the dining table.

"You're in a good mood," he remarked, smiling as he finally put his phone away and ambled closer.

"I am." Blowing out the match, she tipped her face up for his kiss.

"Missed you last night." She'd waited up as long as she could, but ended up falling asleep before he'd gotten back in.

He smiled bigger. "Did you?"

"Mm-hmm," she confirmed.

Beau pulled her into him and kissed her again. "I'm sorry. I stopped by my place for fresh clothes."

Lily chuckled. "Figured you might. Didn't like the ones Aunt Tabitha sent up?"

"They were fine. I just kept thinking they were some kind of charity handout from one of the guys."

"Believe me, no one thinks of you as a charity case. No one has for a very long time."

His cheeks pinkened, and he cleared his throat. "So what's all this?"

"This is a celebration." She pulled back his seat and waved for him to sit.

"What are we celebrating? Your birthday isn't for another three months."

Lily paused for a second with her ass half settled in her own seat. How did he know when her birthday was? Recovering quickly, she took her linen napkin and spread it over her lap. "We are celebrating progress." She poured wine for the both of them, raised her glass for a toast. "To our success, and to Queen Snow. Long may she reign."

Eyes glinting with suppressed laughter, Beau clinked his glass against hers and took a sip. "Okay, what are you up to?"

"Me? Well, I'm glad you asked." As he drizzled dressing over his salad and started eating, she told him all about her impromptu pajama party last night, about her genius idea with the wine, about Amalia's rant and what she thought it might mean.

Beau kept eating, but the longer she spoke, the twinkle in his eye dimmed little by little. And then his easy grin became forced, until it finally fell away altogether. With a clump of salad stuck on his fork, he sat across from her, listening to her ramble on and on.

"So I figured there is one surefire way to get to the bottom of how much she actually knows, so this morning…" She explained about room assignments and surveillance kits, and sat up a little straighter as she proudly told him what she'd done for him.

And that was about the time Beau dropped his fork and exploded out of his seat with, "You did *what!*"

Startled, Lily leaned back as he loomed over her. "What's wrong? I thought you'd be happy."

His eyebrows shot up. "*Happy?* About you putting yourself at risk? And for what!"

"For you, asshole! I was doing you a favor!"

"You requested surveillance equipment from *your own* security! They'll have your name on the sign-out sheet. What happens if housekeeping or, gods forbid, Amalia, or even her client find it in the rooms? What happens if whoever she's with panics?" Counting off on his fingers, he snapped, "You put Amalia in mortal danger, you put your own safety in jeopardy, you—"

"Got you what you never would have gotten on your own," she snapped back, pushing to her feet, not afraid to go toe-to-toe with him. "I made you a fly on the wall so you can see for yourself what Amalia is up to, see the men passing messages back and forth, and hear the messages first-hand. That's what really pisses you off, isn't it? I put together something you hadn't even thought of. The lowly whore managed to outsmart Snow White's mastermind, and you can't handle it, so you're taking it out on me. Well, you know what? *Fuck you, too!*"

Lily stormed around the table, headed for the front door. Beau caught her elbow, pulled her back into him and lifted her off her feet. She screamed, elbowed him, kicked her bare heels back against his shins. She spat out curses, called him names, dug her nails into his arms, and all the while he just stood there and took it, let her rage herself out and never said a word.

Only when she ran out of steam did Beau lower her to her feet, but he still didn't let her go. With his nose in her hair, he said, "You're wrong. I have zero illusions about being any sort of mastermind. I'm just one reasonably smart and incredibly lucky son of a bitch who has a lot of people feeding him information no one else has. And I am so damn proud of what you came up with, it hurts."

"Yeah," she rasped. "I can totally tell how proud you are."

He ignored the outburst, tightening his hold on her. "What upsets me," he said with his mouth against her shoulder, "is the thought that something might happen to you."

She didn't miss the shudder racking through him; he meant what he said. The last of her fight went out of her.

"Lily, I *never* wanted you to be a part of this—I did everything I could to keep you as far from it as possible. The people I go after are the kind who don't blink an eye at putting someone in the hospital for looking at them too long. I have three people in intensive care right now, and I don't even want to think about how much worse it would have been if they didn't know how to fight back and run like hell."

Well, when he put it like *that*…

"What you did is pure genius, but it scares the shit out of me that it might somehow come back to bite you when I'm not there to keep you safe."

"I'm not a hothouse flower," she retorted, wincing when she remembered that was going to be the name of her brothel one day.

"I know you're not," he replied, letting her go so she could face him. "But that doesn't mean I want to see you get hurt."

"So…to recap, I'm a genius, my idea kicks ass, and you have some *serious* communication issues, but you care about me so much that just the thought of me in danger sends you into a panic."

"In a nutshell."

Lily sighed. *What am I going to do with you?*

On Sunday night, Beau sat out on Lily's balcony, still reeling from her reckless initiative. He was proud of himself for managing to smooth things over with her so quickly, and keeping up a mellow facade to boot, but inside he was an unfocused mess.

His instinct screamed at him to get her out of here and into protective custody right away. Just get her gone; change her name, find her a new place to live, and set up 'round-the-clock protection. The gut reaction was so strong, he'd already had to stop himself from texting those instructions to his team five times so far.

Gods, he hadn't felt this on edge since the night Haig had almost died because of him. Just as he had back then, Beau blamed himself for this. He should have seen it coming; should have known Lily wasn't the type to just sit back and let someone else take the bullet. She was too smart for that, and far too fearless for her own good.

The grandfather clock struck ten and music blared out of built-in speakers on either side of the balcony. The people below crowded around immediately, cheering and hooting. *What the fuck?*

Behind him, the bookcase swung open and Lily stepped through, dressed in one of his shirts and a pair of five-inch heels. She struck a pose, tugged her thick-rimmed librarian glasses to the very tip of her nose, and looked over the crowd.

"What are you doing?"

Twisting around to face the back, she struck another pose and said, "I have a show tonight. Did I forget to mention that?" If that wicked smile was any indication, no, she hadn't. She'd chosen not to tell him.

"You can't see me, but I'm scowling at you right now."

Lily grinned and, swaying her hips from side to side, lowered into a crouch. "Oh, yeah, baby. Talk dirty to me."

"*What?*"

She was facing front again, leaning over the railing with her feet apart, her ass in the air. Those below them had a great view right about now, and Beau felt like he was in the middle of a naked-in-public dream. Should he get out of the way? He was invisible, but as hard as everyone was staring at Lily, they sure as hell would notice the wall opening and closing behind her all on its own.

And, dammit, did she have to look so fucking sexy in his shirt?

Lily danced around the balcony, slowly working on the shirt buttons, trusting him to move out of the way so she wouldn't trip. "I want you to watch me," she said, baring one shoulder for the crowd and then coyly pulling the shirt back into place. "I want you to *enjoy* watching me. You get what I'm saying here?"

"Uh, no…"

She stepped away from the railing, put her back against the wall, then slowly slid down its surface into a knees-apart crouch. "Then let me spell it out for you, handsome. Undo your pants and take out that big, hard cock we both know is straining at the seams right now." She undulated her hips, then tipped forward onto her hands and knees and arched her back, tossing her hair over one shoulder. "You're going to pump it and describe it for me. And watch me get wet for you."

Holy shit!

His dick shot so hard, he almost maimed himself getting the zipper down.

Lily purred, sitting back on her heels as she grasped the railing bars and rubbed them up and down, working the crowd below into a frenzy. "I heard that," she told him, then let go of the bars and leaned all the way back until her shoulder brushed his thigh. One hand between her breasts, the other down at her crotch, she writhed and ordered, "Talk to me, Beau. Please."

"I… I can't."

Arching her back, she sat up again, the shirt slipping off her arms to her elbows to reveal a lacy red bra. The crowd went wild. "Why not?"

"Because!"

She hummed thoughtfully, did a little sexy dance number at the railing, and the shirt came off completely. By now, a bunch of people down below were masturbating to the sight of her, both men and women. Beau could tell she got off on it; her skin pinkened, her dance became more sultry, his shirt a handy prop she rubbed all over herself, and damn if he wasn't jealous of a fucking piece of fabric.

And still no words would come. *Fuck!*

Lily twirled around, threw the shirt down and dipped one shoulder, letting the bra strap slide down. "I'm sorry, baby," she said, looking in his general direction. "You did so well the other day, I forgot."

She crouched down again, felt along his legs to place him, then crawled over him. She barely touched him, but the look on her face alone made his balls pull up tight. He groaned when she came down on her elbows, bringing her cleavage against his crotch. "Forgot what?" he managed to say, not recognizing his own voice.

Lily threw her hair back, smiled up at him. "My man is a doer, not a talker." She sat up, straddling his knees, one arm slipped out of the bra strap.

Was she disappointed? *Can't have that.* "Turn around," he said.

She did, managing to make it into a show all on its own. Then her ass was in his lap, her head against his shoulder, and only Beau could hear her panting.

"Now touch yourself."

"Don't have to ask me twice." Lily speared her hand into her panties. As the crowd roared, he reached for her from underneath, adding his fingers to hers, loving the way she cried out, her body shivering over him.

He loved the way the crowd loved it, too. That was one kink he'd never known he had, but he got it now. Understood why Lily didn't want to give it up. What an incredible rush, to be at the center of such heady attention. Lust saturated the air, making him light-headed, hungry for more. Beau could use his tactician brain to control the crowd, make them look where he wanted, do what he wanted; he could keep them on the edge, the way he was doing with Lily, or make them lose their minds, just like Lily, right… *Now.*

Lily cried out, shuddered, and only part of it was for show. The audience began chanting for more, for her to take off the concealing lingerie. "Look at that," she told him. "Look what you're doing to them."

Beau gazed over the crowd, grinning slowly as Lily got to her hands and knees again, pulling away from him to appease them. Her bra came off, and she threw it down to her audience. The screams of eager men reaching for the scrap of fabric deafened Beau. Then a pathetic scuffle broke out over it, until one man emerged the winner.

Beau tensed.

Kincade roared in victory, clutching his prize in a tight fist, then he dropped back into his plush seat and yanked his girl back onto his lap.

"We have a problem," Beau said, instantly on alert.

The girl wasn't Amalia. Amalia wasn't even in the room.

As soon as her show had ended, Lily and Beau went back inside and spent the rest of the night and half of the next day going over the security feeds from Amalia's rooms. Hours and hours of sexplay they couldn't fast-forward through fast enough, and Amalia wasn't in any of it.

Lily double-checked the schedule and, yep, there was Amalia's name assigned to those rooms. But no Amalia. This was bad. Lily knew it, just by looking at Beau. His face was completely blank, that thousand-mile stare scaring her more than anything she'd seen before.

She knew what he was thinking, too. That Amalia had somehow found out what Lily had done and switched rooms at the last minute; that she'd told Kincade and he'd switched tactics again, rubbing it in their faces with his presence in the common room the night before. All of that was possible, but Lily didn't think that's what happened.

"I could just call—"

"No," Beau said before she'd even finished, his posture and facial expression never changing.

"Then what do you want to do?"

He sighed, rubbed his face tiredly. "I don't know." She'd bet her last ducat those weren't words Beau said very often, and that just worried her more. "It's possible we got it all wrong, everything from the very beginning."

"But you don't think so."

"No, that's the thing. All the chatter and all the evidence points to Kincade and whoever he's working for."

"Maybe I'm the one who messed up, and it's not Amalia at all."

"Maybe," he allowed.

"But, again, you don't think so?"

He got up to pace. "It just makes no sense, given everything else we know. My gut tells me she's involved."

"And your gut is never wrong." Because he was Beau Legeare. The new queen and her Rebels had trusted him for a reason, and he's never once let them down—if he had, they wouldn't be alive now.

Beau shook his head. "It's never been before. But then, I've never been this close to an assignment before. Maybe that's the problem. I'm *too* close to it."

Lily shrugged. "Then get a second opinion."

Beau stopped to stare at her. "What?"

"You said it yourself, Beau. You're just a reasonably smart, incredibly lucky son of a bitch who has a lot of people feeding you information no one else has. You don't work alone; that's not your thing. So get someone else to help you."

That blank look came over his face again and he sat back down, staring off into space for so long Lily thought he'd gone into some kind of trance. Then his eyes widened the slightest bit, and he sucked in a surprised breath. "Genius!" He launched at her, kissed her hard, then he had his phone in hand and was closing himself in the bathroom.

"Hey! What did I say about locking a girl out of her bathroom?"

CHAPTER 14

The crowds began to gather in front of Miss Kiki's hours before opening time on Tuesday, queuing up neatly on one side of the walkway, keeping a polite distance from the guards posted in front of the door.

Dozens of beautifully attired people mingled together, their masks firmly in place for an illusion of anonymity but, based on their body language, most of them knew each other quite well.

"What do you think those fripperies cost a body?" one of Beau's men mused through the com piece.

Another snorted. "More than you and I will ever make in our lifetimes."

"Boss, I want a raise."

"Let's keep the lines clear of chatter, shall we?" Beau responded softly. His invisibility charm hid him from sight, but didn't disguise noise. "We wouldn't want to miss anything important."

There was a blessed pause before Penny, the only woman present, spoke up. "I don't get it. What's the point of shelling out that much cash for something you'll just be taking off again anyway? Why even bother dressing at all?"

"Guys!"

The com links went silent. *Thank the gods.*

"Okay, the doors will open in two. Anyone see our mark?"

A chorus of negatives.

"Keep an eye out."

Steam suddenly puffed out from beneath the front door, eliciting a wave of gushing applause. Almost showtime. And still no sign of Chang.

"Heading in to check the interior. Let me know if anything changes."

Beau doubled back to the side service entrance and slipped in after the maid who'd just tossed out a bucket full of kitchen scraps. The bowels of Miss Kiki's were unrecognizable. The heat was cranked up to uncomfortable levels and warm, scented mist sprayed out from strategic locations, creating a dreamy haze effect.

Magical illusions combined with physical props built up a dark, sensuous landscape where anything could happen, and oftentimes did. Beau skirted the stages where actors were just warming up, to the common room which, empty of chairs and tables, was made out as a cushy marshland with satyr-like creatures ready to meet the incoming crowds.

The music started up, the doors opened, and the show began. Beau flattened himself against the wall beside the door to keep out of the way. From this angle, he had a clear view of each invitation the guests handed in. He matched names to masks, memorized the demographic layout, then took careful note of how and where they dispersed.

After the bulk of the crowd made its way inside, a small pause in the flood allowed Beau to tiptoe around the edge of the room to a hidden doorway that would lead him back out into the kitchens. He'd just opened it when his com piece went off again with a new voice: "All right, I'm here. I can't believe I'm here, but I'm here."

Beau slipped inside the tunnel and closed the wall panel almost all the way, leaving just an inch-wide opening to see the front door. There, in the middle of the entryway, with his back straight and his invitation held out between his fore- and middle fingers, stood Beau's brother-in-arms, decked out in all black, with a blood red demon mask covering most of his face.

The ever-stylish, ever-composed Darius Cape-Arrens was a chameleon, capable of blending in anywhere from dockside hovels to royal courts, and not for the first time, Beau envied the ease with which the man could relate to people and manipulate them into trusting him.

Case in point: "Is that *Miss Julianna*?" How the hell had he managed to talk Snow's personal assistant into coming here? How had he even gotten close enough to try? Castle staff was supposed to be off limits, damn it!

"Hey," Darius said, barely moving his mouth. "You have your assignment, I have mine. Now how about we get on with both, eh?"

Not the place, and not the time. Beau swallow back a hot retort and instead said, "Get the lay of the land, then watch for Chang."

"Aye, sir!" Darius retorted, offering Miss Julianna his arm.

Shaking his head, Beau closed the panel and felt his way along the dark passageway. One more player to check on: the tricky Amalia.

Outside the kitchen, the idyllic, fairy tale landscape began to change into more sinister tones of black and red. Not far down the hallway ahead of him was the "underground" demon cave for rough play. He could already hear some interesting sounds coming out of there. Not many people lingered in these parts; it seemed to be either in or out for those particular kinks. Those who had no interest in them quickly moved on.

Beau took a left and skirted the wall across from a couple going at it pretty hard in an alcove to get to Amalia's assigned station. The fairy nest was decorated with oversized feathers padding the bowl of the nest and sparkly crystals hanging from the ceiling. Branches thick enough to support a body or two shot across the room here and there, and all the girls were made up to look as young as possible.

And there was Amalia, sitting on someone's lap and sucking her thumb.

Beau didn't recognize the man she was with, or the other three who circled her like sharks, while two masked female guests played with the other fairy's hair.

"Chang's incoming," one of his men reported. "Three minutes out."

Beau charged back out and almost ran into a giggling group of attendants with their clothes half off, headed toward the game stage.

"Visual confirmation, he's headed for the entry. Wait…"

Beau stopped.

"There's a woman loitering. Gold-black gown, black mask, blonde hair. Anyone got a name?"

A round of negatives.

"He nodded to her. They're going in together."

"Who do we have in the main room?" Beau demanded. "Darius, are you still there?"

"Just left. What do you want me to do?"

Beau raced to the glen. "Stall your date until he gets to you, then herd him toward the back rooms."

"And if he has other plans?"

"Do what you do best," Beau replied, heading for Lily's station. "Change them."

A few minutes into the event and things were already in full swing at the dryad glen. Kendra was on her back by the lagoon with Michael's head buried between her thighs. Their movements were exaggerated, a show to entice the modest observers still in their clothes. The more brazen ones had already stripped and joined in, one woman rubbing her hands all over Michael to get his attention, and a man kneeling by Kendra's face so she could fondle him.

Lily, meanwhile, made her way around the room, giving each observer a few seconds of attention to whet their appetite before moving on to the next. She tugged at cloak laces here, traced a plunging neckline there, arched to each touch and caress. Her skin was painted with a silver sheen and leafy vines twined around her limbs and torso, concealing nothing, yet somehow enhancing her natural beauty. None of the holdouts stood a chance.

"Got Chang as far as the game stage," Darius reported. "The woman with him hasn't said a word yet, but they definitely know each other."

"His wife?" Beau whispered back.

"No. She reminds me of someone, though… Can't think of who."

"Get them over here."

A string of curses followed, then the com link went dead. Darius must have taken out his earpiece. *Shit!*

Beau tiptoed around the room to the curtain of willow branches that hid the exit and slipped out into the night once more. "Perimeter check. Sound off."

His people gave the all-clear one by one.

"Any sign of Kincade?"

"Oh, yeah," Penny said. "I see him. He's camped out one street over by a fancy black limo with tinted windows."

"Did you see him drive in?"

"Negative."

"Run the plates anyway," he ordered.

"Already did. Came back registered to a car-for-hire service. Blake is fighting with them now to get the client records."

"Good work. Keep me posted."

"Aye, sir!" they replied in unison, parroting Darius.

"Chang heading out of the game room," Darius reported.

"Great. Make sure he comes to the dryad glen." Maybe he wouldn't have to make an appearance after all. If Lily could maneuver the judge close to Beau so he could hear what was being said…

He began to feel bad that Miss Marcy had gone to all the trouble of making his costume and mask, until Darius said, "Sorry, buddy, got myself into a bit of a situation here. 'Fraid you're on your own."

Shit. Again. Beau took off at a sprint, tearing off the invisibility charm and securing his mask in place as he rounded to the front of the building. Invitation in hand, Beau cut the fast-moving line of guests between two pairs who'd left a gap of several feet between them. "Did you see him talk to anyone, at least? Make eye contact? Anything?"

When he handed over his invitation at the entrance, the masked butler's eyes went wide at the name on it, but he nodded a bow to usher Beau in without a word.

"Nope," Darius replied. "But he seems very proprietary of his companion. Won't let her two feet from his side."

Could she be his accomplice? Beau pushed through the common room as quickly as he could without drawing too much attention. Difficult to do when he was getting blocked at every turn by eager women running their hands all over him. When one pinched his ass, he realized Miss Marcy might have done too fine a job with his hunter-green tux and beastly mask. "Come on, Darius, give me something here," he pleaded, removing a delicate hand from the fly of his pants.

"Wish I could. He's not making it easy."

Penny's voice chimed in. "Car company gave us a name: Christabelle Pembrooke."

"What do we know about her?"

"Nothing. She's a foreigner."

Beau raised an eyebrow. "Fake name?" If so, then the woman with Chang *was* his contact, and every second they spent together out of Beau's earshot meant evidence down the drain. Easing away the woman trying to lick his ear, he made his voice growly and told her, "Sorry love, I've got a beauty waiting for me in the woods."

"Lucky girl," she sighed, setting him free.

Beau frowned at her, then paused by the back hallway to take a good look around. Every woman near him was staring at him as if she was about to swoon. Had they recognized him? He glanced in a mirror near him to check his mask. He still looked like a fangy beast with magically transformed golden eyes. "Why are they staring?"

"Because you're super hot and look all lickable in your fancy getup," Penny retorted. "Can you stop fishing for compliments now and focus on the mission?"

Choked laughter shook him out of his stunned daze, and he scowled. "Then don't make me wait for answers." He turned down the hallway, wound around couples tittering excitedly about all of the action going on. "Name, Penny. Real or fake?"

"Could be fake," Penny replied. "It'll take time to confirm."

"Time we don't have." Godsdammit! "Get everyone we have on this. I want to know who she is—*now*. Darius, where are you?"

Silence.

Swearing a blue streak, he shoved his way toward the game room, but it was so packed he had no hope of getting inside. A quick survey told him Darius wasn't in the audience, and Beau was about to charge off again, when he did a double take at the stage. "*Gah!*" Squeezing his eyes shut, he stumbled away, but nothing would ever erase the sight of Darius' naked ass pumping back and forth in the midst of a cloud of skirts he recognized as belonging to Miss Julianna.

Shake it off! It's not like you haven't seem him naked before.

That wasn't the point!

Miss Julianna? Snow would kill Darius. Hell, *Beau* would kill him at the first opportunity! What part of "castle staff is off limits" had the man not understood?

Focus. Chang couldn't have gone too far… *There!* Four couples and a satyr performer ahead of him. The woman's gold-black dress stood out like a beacon as she swayed her hips back and forth. They were taking a leisurely stroll past the rooms, peering into each before moving on.

Beau pushed his way forward with an exaggerated stagger, pretending to be drunk off his ass. Only three people between them, walking arm-in-arm and taking up the entire hallway.

Chang turned to his companion, his lips moving as he spoke to her. Beau couldn't read him. The woman smiled in answer, tilting her head in a familiar, angled nod. Where had he seen that gesture before? It tickled his memory, but like Darius, he couldn't…quite…

He sucked in a breath. "Shit."

Over his earpiece, a stunned Penny echoed him. "I know who she is."

"Yeah," Beau murmured, "me, too."

Lily moaned, giving her best impression of being lost for the lover she was riding, but her mind was miles away. Her heart fluttered, her cheeks flushed; she couldn't catch her breath. What was this? Could she be…*nervous?*

No. Not nervous. Petrified. Somewhere in the house, Beau was making his way to the glen, somehow manipulating a traitor and his accomplice into this very chamber without revealing his own identity. She had no active part to play in this spy game; her task was to stay in character and keep the scene alive—just do her godsdamned job and let Beau and his plan take care of the rest.

And she couldn't do it.

She couldn't stop herself from glancing at the doorway, at once anticipating and dreading their appearance. What if she messed something up? What if something went wrong? What if Amalia really was in on all of this, and she found the surveillance equipment and warned Kincade, and they knew they'd been compromised, and all of this was just an elaborate show to keep the rest of them off their scent?

Her masked lover bucked his hips up, and Lily disguised her worried squeak into a sound of pleasure. He was almost done, and two more men with their cocks in hand were already waiting for their turn. Some men didn't like to share.

Another reason why Miss Kiki's Masquerade was so popular: for one night only, the entire house was under a powerful spell to enhance pleasure and prevent any pregnancy or diseases. Men in particular adored it because, as long as they were within these chambers, they could come as many times as they could handle without ejaculating. No downtime between one orgasm and the next. Any other time, they'd pay their weight in gold for that kind of stamina.

Lily raked her nails down her lover's chest to his abdomen, felt him shudder beneath her. Another satisfied customer.

Another glance at the door as she eased up from him, got to her feet and stretched to showcase her body. Ignoring her waiting line, she sashayed her way to the entrance, pretending to be choosing her next lover as she covertly glanced up and down the hallway. No sign of Beau yet. *Gods, where is he?* Had Chang even shown? Why hadn't Beau given her one of those earpieces he'd brought with him? Lily was desperate for an update.

A woman caught her blindly reaching hand and brought it to her corseted breast. Forced to turn her back on the doorway, Lily gave the pretty brunette her warmest smile. She could tell the woman was nervous. Perspiration sheened her upper lip, and her generous breasts quivered with each uneven breath she heaved. A pink tongue slipped out over her lips, but she waited for Lily to make the first move.

Nervous newbies weren't her specialty.

Liar.

All right, *one* nervous newbie was her specialty. But this one made her uncomfortable. The lady was too eager, too excited. The weight of her expectations blazed in her brown eyes, and caused Lily to take an involuntary step away. When painted nails dug into her wrist to stop her retreat, she knew only one course of action would get her out of this without ruining anyone's experience.

Lily returned, cupping the brunette's plump cheeks, and kissed her with slow, languorous laps against her tongue. The lady stopped breathing, her hands quivered as she grasped Lily around the waist. While Lily had her off balance, she maneuvered back into the glen, drawing the lady along toward Kendra. Her foot met the incline of the puddle that served as a lake. Warm water closed in on her ankles, and she kept going, bringing the lady along until her skirts were soaked and only her petticoats kept them from tangling around her legs.

Lily dipped her lips to Brown Eyes' collarbone. Kendra was just behind her, and Lily nudged her sprawled leg with her toe. With her signature move, Kendra arched back from her current lover, and he cried out his pleasure. Moments later, Kendra was behind Lily's brunette, slipping the straps of her shift down her shoulders. The lady's death grip on Lily loosened as Kendra took over.

Lily just bit back a relieved sigh when one of the men put his arms around her from behind, pulling her into him, his hands gripping her breasts hard enough that she had to bite back a wince. She crooned deep in her throat, ran her fingers over his knuckles in a move that usually sufficed to convey her message: *Ease up, will you?*

This time, it had the opposite effect as her would-be lover began thrusting mindlessly against her ass. She leaned back into him, relaxing her body so he had to hold her weight, and he sank down with her. Now she was on her knees and he was bending her forward. He released her breasts to grab her thighs and position them farther apart, but the moment he touched her wet pussy, a harsh curse sounded behind her and he rutted over the curve of her ass, coming before his cock had even entered her.

Lily arched her back, dived underwater to soak herself, then surfaced on the other side, her gaze on the doorway.

Chang!

She'd only ever seen him on TV before, but she recognized that bullish set of his shoulders, the distinct lack of a neck, and the thick hands he liked to curl into ham-sized fists whenever something displeased him. He had the look of a brawler, so incongruous with the distinguished post he held as a supreme judge.

Now, those hands were adjusting the mask of a blonde woman in a gold-black dress. He was talking, but Lily couldn't hear his words. From the brittle smile the woman gave him, though, she didn't like whatever he'd just told her. Either that, or she didn't like him preening her.

He was turning away!

Spurred into action, Lily charged out of the pool, rubbing her wet body for effect as she headed for them. Wouldn't touch Chang with a ten-foot pole. She reached for the woman, instead; caught her delicately gloved hand, just catching the trailing end of Chang's last sentence: "…have to move fast."

But he stopped when his hold on the blonde drew him up short. The lady was now stuck between Chang and Lily, each tugging her in opposite directions. Her eyes looked younger than Lily had first thought. Lily would guess her age at no more than nineteen, if that. What on earth was she doing with a brute like Chang?

Chang turned a black look on them both, and Lily felt an overwhelming urge to get Lady Gold away from him. She didn't have Chang's brutish strength, but she did have her wiles. Smiling, she held up a finger to her lips and winked. With another gentle tug, she turned toward the glen, looking back at Lady Gold over her shoulder.

The girl's pupils had dilated; she was definitely interested. But Chang wouldn't release his hold on her, yanking on her hand hard enough to make her jerk. The brief flash of unease was masked with a low chuckle. "Come, dear, what could it hurt to dally a bit?"

Lily didn't dare look at Chang. She took what she'd gotten and led Lady Gold into the glen, keeping her eyes on the girl's face the entire time. Once inside, Lily immediately reached for her mask, but the blonde turned her face away. *Dammit!*

All right, she'd play along. Ignoring the brute looming behind the girl, blocking her view of the doorway, Lily trailed a wet finger across Lady Gold's exposed chest, then followed a drop of water with her tongue, dipping it into her modest cleavage.

When she came back up, one of those huge hands was circling Lady Gold's throat ever so gently and he was murmuring in her ear. "Yes," Lady Gold said with a breathless quiver. "I understand."

Understand what?

Taking one of Lady Gold's hands, Lily brought it to her naked breast and was rewarded by a coaxed smile, even as Chang grabbed fistfuls of gold-black skirts to yank them up. "I like this side of you, pet," Chang said. "Quid pro quo. Now why did I never think of that?"

Lady Gold jerked against Lily as Chang thrust into her, her face pinched with pain.

Lily wanted to murder him.

CHAPTER 15

Lady Thessaly McCrane.

Gods, not this again! Beau's conviction was now absolute. There was no way Chang could plead innocence in any way after this. Not when he kept company with the very young widow of the late Lachlain McCrane.

Beau still had nightmares about how close Snow had come to losing everything on the very day that should have solidified her victory. He'd never forget how the white-marbled coronation room had been stained red with the blood of Zorana's militiamen.

McCrane had financed them in secret, even as Zorana's royal armies had fallen one battalion at a time. He'd let the enemy into the castle; exploited a single unguarded moment, thinking to slay a defenseless lamb, not realizing the power of the rightful queen's fury until she'd unleashed it on him in full force.

In the end, McCrane had lost his head to the guillotine after suffering a humiliating loss. His child bride, however, had been judged innocent of his misdeeds and allowed to retain her title and any property endowed to her by her family. At seventeen years of age to McCrane's forty-two, newly married and miserable, she'd passed the truthsense interrogation so well, Beau had *apologized* to her afterward for putting her through it.

Had he been wrong?

Chang and Lady McCrane were at the doorway to the dryad glen. More words passed between them, a terse interchange, by the looks of it, then Chang took Lady McCrane's hand and began pulling her away.

No!

The people in front of him stalled, undecided. The hallway around the glen was almost as crowded as the game room, with people all but hopping in place to take a turn inside. Beau couldn't get through them without causing a stir. They were getting away!

Then Lily herself lunged soaking wet out of the glen just in time to catch Lady McCrane's hand and draw her back inside. Looking like his head would start steaming, Chang followed after her.

Now there was a pissed-off, possibly violent traitor in the same room with a naked, defenseless Lily.

Beau shoved his way between the couple directly in front of him so hard the man slammed into the wall, the woman stumbling into him. People in the doorway. His fists clenched tight, ready for a fight, even as the last smidgen of his rational mind screamed that he was fucking up the mission.

Didn't matter.

Lily was in trouble. *Nothing else* mattered.

Beau was about to start throwing punches, his team shouting over each other in his earpiece, when a hand snagged his arm, drawing him into a naked, male torso. He had a split second to recognize Michael's face before the man stuck his tongue into Beau's mouth. Shocked out of his rage, Beau froze.

Michael broke away, his fingers digging into Beau's shoulder as he pulled him through the crowd into the glen. "Hello, lover," he purred, but his expression was tense. "What took you so long?"

"Got held up," Beau replied blankly. *What the hell...?*

"Stop!" Lily suddenly cried. "Get the fuck off her!"

Beau's head whipped around to see her holding on to Lady Mc-Crane as Chang rutted on the poor girl from behind. Lily shoved at him, but there was little she could do while holding Lady McCrane, and the sick fuck took advantage, using his weight to force the two women off balance. They fell back into the pool, Lily on the bottom.

An animalistic roar made Beau's ears ring, and then he was on top of Chang, hauling him away, bodily throwing the bastard against the discombobulated onlookers.

Blood in the water. Lily's? Beau grasped Lady McCrane's arms, pulling her up as Lily surfaced, sputtering. She shook her hair out of her face, met eyes with Beau, then took in the girl's condition. Before Beau could react, she shot to her feet and launched herself at Chang like a screeching banshee.

Chang yelled out, then hauled off and backhanded Lily so hard she fell sideways.

"Lily!"

"Fucking whore," Chang snarled. His mask was askew, his face scratched to hell and back.

Beau shoved Lady McCrane into Michael's arms and launched himself at Chang. The judge's pugilistic fists connected with Beau's sides like sledgehammer blows. Beau didn't feel a thing past the haze of a blood rage. For each hit he took, he delivered two—and he fought dirty. Despite his weight advantage, Chang went down in seconds, shouting obscenities, spraying bloody spittle, until Beau hammered his face with a quicksilver series of punches to shut him up.

People screamed. His peripheral vision filled with flashes of colorful fabrics as the women fled. Men shouted for security, for someone to get the madman off the guy. Beau kept driving his fist into Chang's face again and again until he heard a satisfying *crack*. And still, no one stepped up to stop him.

Chang's arms fell limp to his sides, his mouth went slack and his head lolled as Beau continued his relentless assault. *As long as he breathes…*

Multiple sets of strong arms hauled him up and away. He fought them, beyond comprehending the words being shouted at him as he struggled against his captors, single-mindedly intent on ending the son of a bitch who'd hurt Lily. Someone approached Chang, checked his pulse, slapped his face. Chang roused with a pained moan, and Beau redoubled his efforts to get free.

Suddenly, Lily was there, standing in front of him. Her eyes were wild, pupils dilated. Her cheek was darkening with a bruise, but her voice was calm, soothing when she laid her hand against his chest and spoke the words that finally began to pierce the murderous haze. "Beau, I'm okay. You have to stop now. Please, Beau, you're scaring me."

Just like that, Beau stopped fighting. She crooned to him, drew closer. Shaking with a desperate need to touch her, he held up his bloody hands to signal he was finished. They released him by degrees and as soon as he was free, Beau snatched Lily to him, crushed her in his arms.

"It's okay," she was saying into his chest. "I'm okay. It's over."

The haze cleared by slow degrees. He breathed in deeply, comforted as much by the feel of Lily safe in his arms as he was by the way she clutched him back as hard as she could. Only then did he regain enough sense to survey the rest of the scene.

Chang sat up against the far wall, with Darius standing over him. Michael had found a blanket somewhere and bundled it around the weeping Lady McCrane.

With their masks torn off, the rest of their audience recognized the Rebels at once, and a scandalized hum swept through the crowd. Kendra took charge, herding guests out of the room, calling for house security, and a healer for Lady McCrane, who had grown eerily silent.

Kendra managed to push everyone back as far as the hallway, but they wouldn't move a step beyond that, all of them craning their necks to see the show's finale.

Which now amounted to the utter ruination of Beau's mission.

Chang appeared to realize that at the same time. He sought Beau through rapidly swelling eyelids and gave him a bloodied grin. "Worth it to see you righteous fuckers fall. Enjoyed that scuffle, did you? Over a fucking *whore*? You just threw your career down the shitter, boy. Soon as I get my mug healed up, I'll see you in court for damages. You've got *nothing*."

Which was as good as an admission that there had been something to *get*. Before Beau had fucked it up. They didn't have enough to arrest him, and the son of a bitch knew it. He was gleefully rubbing it in their faces.

"N-not true," Lady McCrane said, drawing Beau's attention to her.

Lily nudged him to be set free. Tightening his hold to tell her in no uncertain terms that she would be staying put until he'd deemed the situation contained, Beau turned sideways so they could both face the young woman. Her small frame shivered, her teeth chattered, and she wouldn't meet anyone's gaze, but there was a stubborn set to her chin, even as she shrank into the safety of Michael's side.

"Action outside," Penny piped in through his earpiece, just as Chang's gleeful expression turned murderous.

"Go on," Beau said, addressing both Penny and Lady McCrane.

"You shut your fucking mouth!" Chang roared.

Darius stepped in front of him, blocking his view of the young woman as Penny quickly responded, "A shit-ton of half-naked people running for the hills. One of 'em looks like that girl you had us keep an eye out for."

Amalia.

"You won't squawk," Chang said with a careless chuckle, but his limbs were rigid with tension. "You'd be just as culpable." Another admission. And still not enough to charge him.

"Lady McCrane," Darius intoned, keeping an eye on Chang, "you have a singular opportunity to make a deal. I'm sure Queen Snow can show leniency, under the circumstances."

"She's heading for Kincade," Penny reported. "Yep. Confirmed, she just ran up to Kincade in a tizzy."

"Bag them both," Beau murmured to her in an aside and dismissed her at once, his attention on the rapidly blanching Chang.

"Rest assured, the guilty party will be made to pay," Darius added smoothly. "For *all* his crimes."

Lady McCrane looked hesitant, but then her chin raised a notch higher and she looked Chang dead in the eye. "I'll tell you everything you want to know. Dates, contacts, account numbers, everything. I'll give you my husband's ledgers—" Her sentence cut off on a scream as Chang snarled, surging to his feet, roaring like an enraged bull.

Beau was already turning to shield Lily with his own body when Darius coldcocked the judge with a swiftness Beau had seen many times in the past and, before he'd even made it fully to his feet, Chang dropped back down. He wouldn't be getting up again any time soon.

Just then, a commotion outside ushered in the proprietress, draped in a crimson silk gown, her black mask clutched in one hand. Miss Kiki took in the scene, lingering on Chang, then narrowed her eyes at Lily, still in Beau's arms. "How dare you," she hissed.

Hearing her aunt's voice, Lily extricated herself from Beau to face her. "Auntie—"

"And on the night of my ball! My patrons are scattering to the winds, and you dare stand there and call me *auntie!*"

Lily gaped at her. In all the times Beau had seen Miss Kiki circulate among her precious patrons, she'd never been anything but pleasant and flirtatious. Now, she looked as if she would physically attack her own niece for ruining her shindig. Beau stepped up, pulling Lily behind him. "It's not her—"

"What is the rule, girl?" Miss Kiki demanded, loud enough that even people out in the hall quieted to hear every word. "*Never* bring your lover into my house!" She sneered, as if the very sight of her niece disgusted her. "Pack your bags. I want you out by morning."

Beau felt Lily shudder next to him. "Aunt—"

"I said *get out!*"

Whispers hissed through the remaining crowd of onlookers as Lily stared at her aunt, the only family she had. Miss Kiki's stone-cold facade never wavered; that imperious, pointing finger never lowered. Squaring her shoulders, Lily raised her chin proudly, but her movements were wooden as she walked out, brushing past her aunt so hard it set Miss Kiki back a step. She never looked back.

When she was gone, Miss Kiki spared one more scathing look at those left behind, lingering on Michael, still holding Lady McCrane. "Clean this place up." When she swept out of the room, the crowds parted before her as if she were on fire.

"Please," Lady McCrane whimpered. "Please, get me out of here."

Darius took one look at Beau and said, "Royal guard is probably already on the way. I'll take it from here."

Sparing the man a nod, Beau tore the com piece out of his ear and loped off after Lily.

CHAPTER 16

Tears blurred Lily's vision and her hands shook so hard it took her three tries to get the door unlocked, but she refused to fall apart. No way would she give her aunt that kind of satisfaction. Yet as she wiped her face and stepped into her cozy little apartment, her determination faltered and she froze just past the threshold.

Miss Kiki's wasn't just her home, it was her family, and her job, too—it was everything. How was she supposed to leave it all behind? Where would she go? She stared into space, teetering on the verge of succumbing to mindless panic. If she allowed it to take hold, it would never let her go.

But falling apart now was not an option. As painful as it would be to leave Miss Kiki's, Lily had weathered far worse. This was nothing. A minor setback.

Lily would clear out, just like her aunt demanded.

But oh, how she would make her regret it. Yes, revenge was exactly what Lily needed. None of this woe-is-me bullshit.

Marching across the living room, she dragged the steamer trunk away from the wall, threw open the lid, and surveyed the space with a strategic eye. The essentials would be coming with her tonight, just in case her aunt got it in her head to get even pettier and trash her stuff to make room for her next protégé. The rest, she'd have to send for, because once she'd stepped foot out that door, Lily was never, *ever* coming back.

Aunt Tabitha wanted to kick her out even though she knew full well that none of what'd happened had had anything to do with her relationship with Beau? Fine. Lily could be just as petty. She'd pick up that gauntlet and use it to bitch-slap the hell out of her aunt. Tabitha thought Lily would give her some healthy competition? *Ha!* Lily would *bury* her. In two years' time, people in Kesteran would be asking, "Miss Kiki, who?"

Her favorite quilt and pillows went into the trunk, followed by the stack of magazines and torn-out pages she'd saved in a shoebox. No knickknacks to speak of, but she did have a gorgeous wooden swan poised in mid-ascent Aunt Tabitha had gifted her one year.

Lily punted it across the room.

"Whoa!" Beau ducked in the doorway, and the swan flew over his head, down the hidden stairwell.

"Sorry," she mumbled, making a mental note to find him later and apologize, but right now her time was short and her mind was otherwise occupied. The trunk already overflowed. Did she have another suitcase somewhere? In the closet, maybe?

She rounded the couch and headed for the bedroom.

Move out, move on, make her pay.

That was the plan. What happened between that A, B, and C she would figure out later. She had to get her shit together first before she could focus on where to move it.

Her closet was meticulous, arranged by categories and color-coordinated. She didn't own much, but what she had was expensive, and made to order. Lily had enjoyed Marcy's personal attention as one of the perks of being the proprietress' niece, and it brought her a spiteful kind of joy to carefully remove each item of custom clothing off its hanger to take with her. *Thanks for the wardrobe, Auntie.*

Buzzing in her ear. She ignored it.

With her arms full of clothes, she searched the back corner. No suitcases to be found there. Not even a handbag. Lily shrugged. The bedsheet would have to do. She'd make a bundle, like she'd done back when Miss Kiki's had burned down.

She should probably put some clothes on first, though.

Setting her burden down on the floor, Lily took a folded track suit off the top to put on. It was crimson, the perfect color to compliment her current mood. The black sneakers would go well with it, too.

More buzzing.

Lily shook it off, carrying armfuls of clothes past the obstruction in her path to the bed. She went around it again on the way back for her bedding and towels. Another perk of Miss Kiki's, not to be left behind: linens to make even the queen jealous. Yeah, they were definitely coming with her.

Move out, move on, make her pay. Lily had no idea where she was supposed to move out to, but she could probably go crash at a hotel or something. Hell, Beau had survived most of his childhood living on the streets; Lily could hack it for a day or two until she found new digs. She had the money—

"*Lily!*"

She blinked, focusing on the green thing in her path. "Oh, hey, Beau." *He's still here?* She'd thought the flying swan had sent him running. Didn't men usually avoid women when they were in a state? *Tunnel vision, girl.* The only way to get anything done was to focus. Three easy steps: *Move out, move on, make her pay.* Anything else had to be put on the back burner, or she'd never make it out of here without falling to pieces.

"'Hey, Beau?' That's all? Did you even hear anything I just said?"

Lily brushed past him on the way to the bathroom. "Uh, no, not really. Don't have time to chat. Night's almost over and Aunt Tabitha wants me out by morning. Got packing to do."

He sighed. "Anything I can do to help?"

"Yeah, grab that fluffy throw, will you?" Her toiletries were almost depleted. *Shit.* Could she sneak some out of the supply room? It couldn't be a bigger offense than a fired office worker stealing staplers and paper clips, right? Besides, after all the years she'd worked here, the veritable *fortune* she'd made for Miss Kiki's, in money and prestige, Lily was owed a decent severance package.

She'd raid some of the better stuff on her way out. Everyone would be busy cleaning up downstairs, anyway. They'd never notice. "Oh, umm, sorry about your mission." She dropped an armful of odds and ends into the center of the bed and paused long enough to really look at Beau. He was clutching the fluffy throw and looking at her like she imagined someone would at a wild predator that had wandered into their backyard and gotten its paw stuck in a trap: pitiful, but wary.

"Don't worry about that, we'll get it figured out. I'm more concerned about you right now. Are you okay?" He was really asking how much she was *not* okay.

Lily looked at him, searched for that secret thing she desperately needed to see in his eyes, and found nothing.

He still didn't care. Not in the way she needed him to. Downstairs in the glen, Beau had clutched her to his chest as if someone would have to forcibly pry her away for him to ever let her go, and for just a moment, she'd felt so… so…

Cherished.

Yes, that was the exact right word for it. She'd felt completely cherished. Lily had soaked it up like sunshine; had almost made herself believe that they'd made progress, that maybe Aunt Tabitha had been on to something and the two of them might actually have a chance together.

Apparently, that had all been just a heat-of-the-moment thing, because the man standing before her now was nothing more than a polite stranger. His words were the right ones, but the sentiment behind them was all wrong. Careful distance, guarded gaze… He wasn't asking as a lover; he was asking as the right hand of the queen, assessing collateral damage after a botched operation.

That's me. Collateral.

Scope of damage: total.

The seasoned seductress had fallen head over heels for the rebel with a heart of gold, and not an inch of space in it to spare for her. And just as she'd expected, it hurt so much she couldn't breathe, let alone answer him. How she managed to stay standing, Lily would never know, but if she was going to have any chance in hell of walking out of here, she had to do it fast.

So she squared her shoulders and fortified her sagging spine. "I'm fine." *I'm dying.* "My head aches a bit, but it's not bad." *My heart is shattered and I'll never set it right again. Why can't you see it?*

Beau looked like he would round the bed and come to her, and Lily almost wished he would. But he stopped himself, crushing the fluffy throw in a white-knuckled grip before handing it over. "You should see a healer before you go."

Tiny heart shards bursting into flame. "Noted," she choked out. "Will do." With the throw spread on top of the pile to keep it all contained, she tugged one corner of her bedsheet free with numb fingers, grateful for anything that saved her from having to meet his gaze.

Lily felt Beau watching her. His silence gnawed so much, she couldn't stand it. "I've got enough money saved up to start over." Years of commissions and tips that she'd never spent. A small fortune to invest however she pleased. *See? Not a charity case.* "I'll check into a hotel for the night, and tomorrow I'll start hunting for a place of my own."

"You could stay with me."

Lily paused at the second corner, sheet clutched in her hand so hard she felt the weave start to warp. She held her breath. *Say it. Say you want me with you.*

"I-I mean, this is all my fault. If I hadn't dragged you into it…"

He kept talking, but Lily didn't hear the rest. Gods, how much more could she take? "Forget it," she said, yanking out the corner and throwing the sheet over the pile of things in the middle. "It's okay. You were on a mission for the crown. I'm sure I can appeal for damages or something. I'll figure it out. You don't have to go out of your way."

"Oh." Beau's cheeks flushed beet red as he stuffed his hands into his pockets, shoulders hunched up to his ears. Now *he* couldn't meet *her* gaze, and the twisted part was, she couldn't even get mad at him. As pissed as she was at Tabitha, she couldn't be angry with Beau. She hurt. Unbearably. But she wasn't mad. Beau had never lied to her. He'd never promised anything—in fact, he'd gone out of his way to make sure she understood that their time together was limited. The presumptions were all Lily's. Her own fault.

Dammit, he *was* a good guy! A great guy, who'd probably worship the ground his future wife walked on. Why couldn't it be her? Was her line of work really *that* objectionable to him? He hadn't seemed to mind when he'd used it for his own benefit.

That at least brought Lily enough healthy resentment to keep her upright as she skirted around him, to work on the other side of the bed. "Not a damsel in need of saving, remember?"

"Lily, that's not what I meant. Will you please just look at me?"

And endure even more well-meaning kiss-offs? No. Lily might only be a whore, but she was still human, and she could only tolerate so much pain before her soul simply gave up. It was time to make a strategic retreat, lick her wounds, and figure out a way to forget that, while the last two weeks had been the happiest of her entire life, they'd been nothing but a pleasant vacation for Beau.

Tying off the corners, she hauled the bundle off the bed and over her shoulder. "No time. Told you, I gotta be out by morning."

"Yes, but you don't have to—"

"You want to help? You can get the door and call down for a car. I can take it from there."

None of it meant a thing.

Lily wouldn't even look at him, as if she'd already closed the book on what had happened and moved on. That easily, she shut Beau out of her life, and she couldn't seem to get away from him fast enough.

The speech he'd prepared died a silent death in his mind. Every logical argument about why it would make sense for her to move in with him, and how good they were together, and all the reasons why all other courses of actions were a waste of time because they'd just end up together again down the line anyway, were just an exercise in futility.

Because Lily didn't care. She'd allowed him into her life for a brief time as…what? Her duty to the crown? And why not make the best of it by enjoying each other, rather than awkwardly getting in each other's way? It made sense, logically. And naïve idiot that he was,

Beau had actually thought it'd meant something more.

You're a fool. You've been a fool for ten years, and you're an even bigger fool now. Because now he knew exactly what he was missing. What he'd been missing for ten fucking years by not having the balls to tell the woman who haunted his dreams that he wanted her.

Except now he knew it wouldn't have mattered anyway, because brave, beautiful, clever Lily had no room in her vibrant, hedonistic life for a straight-and-narrow stick-in-the-mud like him. Beau had thought he'd made her happy in the last two weeks, brought her pleasure—surely, she would have told him otherwise. Apparently, it hadn't been enough.

And Beau had nothing else to offer her that she might want. A warm, safe home? She'd just go out and get one. A respectable name? Lily took pride in her own, in the reputation she'd built for herself as one of the best, and she had no intention of giving it up. She shouldn't; Beau didn't want her to. He just wanted to be the one she came home to at the end of the night.

Not a damsel in need of saving. A nice way of saying, "You're not wanted."

There had to be a way to make her understand that he didn't *want* to save her; he just didn't want to say goodbye again. Ever.

But this wasn't the time. Lily was clearly upset, and he seemed to be saying all the wrong things, making everything worse. Beau needed time to regroup and really plan out a proper course of action. This was too important to botch with impulsive word vomit, and he was too worked up to come up with a good save.

"Here, give me your phone."

Lily scowled, readjusting the heavy bundle over her shoulder. He wanted to take it for her, but she'd just slap him for his efforts. "Why, you want to program your number into it, in case I need a hero in the middle of the night?"

Beau winced. Heat flushed up his neck and face again; he started sweating under his collar. "I'm not listed. You won't have a way to contact me. And I'm assuming you'll want to bill me for the last two weeks?" Her lips pressed together in a thin line. He didn't know how to interpret that. "I was going to give you my email address."

After a long, wordless stare, Lily dropped her burden, rolled her shoulder, and looked around the room. Her phone was on the dresser by the window; she'd almost walked out without it. Crossing to it, she typed in her code and slapped it into his outstretched hand. "Hope you're prepared for a lot of OT."

Beau punched in his email, then added his home and mobile numbers for good measure. "Do your worst," he said, handing it over. Whatever she asked for, it'd never be enough to pay back what she'd done for him. So why did he feel like it was all wrong to even discuss it? "And, for what it's worth, I'm sorry. For everything."

Her shoulders sagged as she closed her eyes. Exasperated? "Godsdammit, Beau. Why can't you just…" She didn't finish.

"Just what?" Whatever it was, he'd do it. "Tell me," he said. *Tell me what to do to convince you to stay.*

When Lily opened her eyes, they glittered with tears and Beau felt as if he'd been whaled in the chest with a six-ton sledgehammer. Unable to help himself, hating this distance between them, he stepped up to close it. She didn't back away. "Tell me what you want." She'd never hesitated before, and he desperately needed her to guide him now. Beau was flying blind here.

Lily gazed at him for a long moment, looking as lost as he felt. He sensed hesitation in her, which baffled him. Between the two of them, Lily had never been the shy one.

"Tell me," he said again, taking one more step to bring him almost toe-to-toe with her. She had to crane her head back to hold his gaze, and her eyelids naturally lowered the smallest bit. He needed to kiss her more than he needed his next breath, but he held back, terrified of making a mistake. Painfully aware that one more would send her running so fast, he'd never catch up.

Her lips parted to speak, and he held his breath, hands fisting at his sides to keep from touching her.

A loud pounding on the door startled them apart. "Lily! Are you in here?" Peter. And he'd brought Steve and Erick with him, too. Beau bit back a foul curse as Lily went to meet them in the living room.

"We heard what happened," Erick said. "I'm so sorry."

"Yeah," Steve added. "That was a dick move on your aunt's part."

"Anything we can do to help?" Peter asked, nodding to Beau in acknowledgment. The only one to do so.

Lily raked her fingers through her wet hair. "Uh, I think I got all the important stuff packed. If you want to give me a hand carrying it down." She'd accept their help, but not Beau's? Of course. *They* were her friends. Beau didn't even rank that high.

Erick and Steve took up the steamer trunk between them and carried it out right away. No questions asked. Peter lingered, seeming to realize there was something more going on here than met the eye. "Where are you gonna go?"

"Hotel for now. The rest, I'll figure out later. Tell your bitch boss she'd better not throw out my furniture. I'll send for it in a few days. She owes me that much, at least."

Casting an awkward glance at Beau, Peter said, "I have a spare bedroom in my place, if you want to crash with me."

If she agreed, Beau might just have to murder the man.

"That's sweet of you to offer, but I can't. I need to be on my own for a little while. Figure some shit out." She didn't even look at Beau. He might as well have ceased to exist. *You're not wanted, remember?*

Beau cleared his throat. "Here, don't forget your phone." He handed it over, keeping his expression carefully blank. *Have to play this right. Play it cool.* "If you need anything, give me a call."

"I will," she said, matching his nonchalant tone. Beau waited for her to say more, but she didn't, and the silence stretched on awkwardly until Peter frowned at him and mouthed, *What the hell?*

Wish I knew, man. "Well, good night." Somehow, he managed to turn away and walk out the door. Somehow, he managed not to trip on the stairs. Somehow, he found himself outside of Miss Kiki's, walking down the street with no idea of how many people he'd passed on the way, or what they'd said to him.

Dawn was breaking in the east in a cast of gray that spread up from the city skyline and doused the flickering stars one by one. The lighter the day became, the darker it felt until, by the time Beau had opened the front door of his house, he felt as if he was stepping right back into the deepest, darkest cavern of the Rebels' old mine.

And his last candle didn't want anything to do with him.

CHAPTER 17

The following week kept Beau so busy he hardly had time to sleep. By Wednesday, he was gulping down coffee by the pot and muttering to himself worse than he'd done during the war.

True to her word, Lady McCrane had testified against Judge Chang, and handed over a veritable trove of information they could have used a year ago, including a roster of all members of the sleeping resistance. Half of that roster had fallen in the coronation day attack, but Beau and his team had tracked down the rest and all were now either imprisoned or under investigation. Anyone else in any way connected to them would be suspect, and subject to searches and questioning, which gave Beau and his team a new roster of dozens of names to keep eyes on.

After Lady McCrane's testimony, Chang's homes—all four of them—had been searched. They'd discovered documentation on all the secret bank accounts and shell companies he'd used to profit off his knowledge as one of Snow's trusted council members, as well as letters from Zorana, instructing him on how and when to use them. Irrefutable proof of his guilt, which meant an official sentencing was only a formality at this point and the guillotine was already being prepared for Judge Chang's execution on Sunday night. Time enough to conclude the trial, carry out the sentence, spread the word throughout the kingdom, and give Chang a day to come to terms with his fate.

As for the co-conspirators, Kincade and Mr. Menu both got life sentences for their part in the ploy, which included blackmail against Lady McCrane to force her compliance. Amalia managed to skate by with two years because, as it turned out, she really was just a clueless ditz out to make a little extra money. To Beau's knowledge, no one at Miss Kiki's was all that surprised, or overly broken up over it—

"You do know you have the entire castle staff at your disposal now, don't you?"

Breaking off mid-mutter, Beau looked up from the report in front of him to squint at the man leaning against his doorjamb. Instead of shoving to his feet, as he ought to do in the presence of the king, Beau scowled. "Don't remind me." More people working meant more reports Beau had to go over on a daily basis. He'd already had to hire five extras to shoulder the work, which wouldn't be abating for the foreseeable future. He refused to let another lead slip through his fingers, no matter how innocent they might appear.

King Marcus chuckled, shaking his head. He was a poster child for all Princes Charming of the world: tall, built, fashionable, with a face handsome enough to inspire pop songs. It'd be easy to hate the man if he was nothing more than a handsome face, but in truth, King Marcus also had a keen intelligence behind those deep brown eyes and a big heart that loved their queen above and beyond anything else, including reason and his own life. Which was why the Rebels had allowed him to live, let alone marry her.

Marcus came up to Beau's desk, eyed the stack of binders on the chair facing it, then shoved it all to the floor and sat. "You look like hell."

"Thank you," Beau replied. "Are you here for the McCrane report?"

Marcus scoffed. "Have you ever seen me read a report in my life?"

No, Beau had not. Yet somehow, Marcus always seemed to know everything going on behind the scenes anyway. "Then tell me what Snow's decided to do with Lady McCrane."

Marcus shrugged. "She may have obstructed the investigation a year ago, but as mired as the girl was in the conspiracy, she is still innocent of any willful act against the crown. We decided to strip her of her title and all remaining holdings, and banish her from Valefort."

Then Snow had shown leniency, just as Darius had promised. "Good."

"I'm glad you approve," the king replied with a twitch of his lip. "Does that satisfy your need for business talk, or do you need to discuss more before we get down to it?"

Beau frowned. "Down to what?"

Marcus leaned forward, bracing his elbows on his knees. *Uh-oh.* "Beau, you're a guy who appreciates straight-talk over beating around the bush, so I'll be blunt." And he paused, hesitating. When Marcus rubbed his mouth in frustration, Beau knew nothing good would come of this discussion.

"Are you trying to tell me I'm fired?"

Marcus' brown-eyed gaze snapped to him. "*What?* Why the hell would I want to fire you?"

Beau flushed. "I almost botched the mission." Not *almost.* He *had* botched it. If not for Chang's massive ego and Lady McCrane's willingness to testify, Chang would have walked, thumbing his nose at them the entire way.

"Ah, yes. I do want to talk about that mission. But not for the reasons you're thinking."

"Well, now I'm officially confused."

"Believe me," Marcus retorted. "We know."

"What's that supposed to mean?"

"Dude, my wife sent you—a *virgin*—to camp out at a brothel that just so happened to be the home of the girl you'd been carrying a torch for for a *decade.* You come out, she's fired, you disappear into your office, and we don't hear a peep from you for a week. Don't get me wrong, I love that meddlesome woman like nobody's business, but this mission she sent you on had even me scratching my head."

"Wow, you weren't kidding about being blunt."

Marcus huffed out a breath, clearly uncomfortable with this discussion. "I just figured you might want to talk to someone. You know, in case you had any—*ahem*—questions. About what happened. Or how to proceed."

Was it possible for a person to actually die of embarrassment? Beau would have thought if it hadn't happened in the last few weeks, he'd be immune, but this "conversation" was pushing even those limits.

When Beau didn't reply right away, Marcus said, "I think we can both agree that we'd rather be anywhere else right now, doing literally anything other than talking about this."

"Vehemently, yes."

"Yeah, thought so," he muttered. "But as painfully awkward as it is, I'm still gonna ask, because I consider you my friend, and that's what friends do." A pause. "*Do* you want to talk about it?"

Beau took a deep breath. "No."

"You understand that the offer stands indefinitely?"

Beau nodded. "Yes." And for both of their sakes, he would never be taking him up on it.

"Cool." Marcus pushed to his feet and all but ran for the door, tossing a "See ya" over his shoulder.

Beau stared at the empty doorway for a long time. He appreciated the effort on Marcus' part more than he could say, but the point remained that there was absolutely nothing to talk about where Lily was concerned. She hadn't reached out to him a single time this entire week—he'd been checking his email compulsively every five minutes just to make sure he hadn't missed it.

She'd officially moved on. Without him.

Part of the reason why he'd thrown himself into the task of cleaning up this mess around Chang was to keep his mind occupied enough not to think of her. Some minutes it worked better than others. In the brief lulls, when he put away one report and took up another, he couldn't help thinking about what she might be doing at that very moment. He often found himself staring at a paragraph he'd already read five times without seeing it, imagining what Lily might have thought of all this. What clues she might have caught that he'd missed.

Beau tortured himself nightly, remembering their time in her apartment, ensuring he wouldn't sleep a wink for hours to come. And when he did manage to fall asleep, he always woke up less than an hour later, reaching for her across his empty bed.

For most of his life, Beau'd had no one; had contented himself with his own company; had even kept a cautious distance from his comrades-in-arms, expecting them any day to just walk away and never look back. After two weeks of sleeping with Lily, he'd become so used to her presence, he couldn't function without it. He questioned his every decision, when he never had before. His famous, infallible gut instinct was now nothing more than a hollow, knotted ache in his stomach.

Rubbing his weary eyes, he put on another pot of coffee, then surveyed the mess Marcus had left on the floor. Those files were already closed, Beau just needed to find a place to archive them. Only one of his office cabinets still had a bit of available space. The files in it were so old, the pages had darkened around the edges and the print had faded.

They were the first reports he'd ever compiled for Snow, smudged with coal from the mine and still smelling faintly of smoke. He'd kept them even after they'd all been scanned and archived digitally, so he'd never forget where they'd all begun. So he'd remember never to let any of them sink that far again.

The files had no place in this office anymore. Time to retire them permanently. Pulling out one tattered cardboard cover after the other, he piled them all on the floor next to the recycling bin. The last file bound a stack of papers in different sizes and thicknesses. It almost fell apart in his hands when he picked it up, and as he juggled the haphazard, four-inch thick pile, something clattered out of it and across the floor.

Beau froze, staring down at a pair of dice so worn the dots were chafed almost clean off. The feel of old paper in his hands, the smell of smoke, those dice... He blinked and he was nineteen years old again, staring into space as Lily scampered away as if she hadn't just rocked his world on its axis with one innocent kiss.

Beau's mouth quirked in a bitter smile. Ten years later, not much had changed. Was he forever doomed to want a woman who didn't want him back?

His computer chirped with a new message alert. He dropped the file and shoved to his feet, swiping up the dice along the way. There was a new message in his inbox from lilypad69 with no subject line. Heart in his throat, he hesitated before clicking it open.

The body simply said:

**Please submit payment within 14 days of receipt.
Thank you for your business.**

Lily Maverick

And there went his heart, plunging down into his stomach. She hadn't even bothered with a personal message.

Beau scrolled down across the invoice to the final figure at the bottom. It was the largest amount he'd ever had to pay for anything in his entire life, yet still far less than he'd expected. Was she playing with him again? He'd heard the girls at Miss Kiki's quoting their prices left and right. Using those as a basis for comparison, and multiplying by two weeks' worth of time, Lily hadn't charged him even a third of what the final figure should amount to, not even counting room, board, and his tailored costume for the masquerade.

The invoice had a link to a payment page. If he submitted the sum, they'd officially be done. Loose ends tied off, formalities out of the way, nothing more for either of them to say to each other. Beau didn't like it. He liked it even less that she'd obviously lowballed him.

Shoving away from the table, he rattled the dice in his fist as he paced back and forth. Over the last week, he'd thought up a thousand different scenarios to manipulate one more meeting between him and Lily, a thousand different things he could say to her. He'd rejected a thousand more, and still the *right* thing to say eluded him.

Beau crouched down in front of a stretch of wall incongruously bare of any shelves or stacks of paper. He rattled the dice again and threw them. The shaved, wooden cubes bounced off the wall and rolled back toward him, settling, as they usually had, on a six and a one.

If he paid the invoice, she would disappear. If he didn't, she might send authorities to collect, but Beau doubted she would bother making the trip herself.

Suddenly, he lit on what might just be the most brilliant idea he'd ever come up with. He rushed back to the computer, clicked the PAY NOW button and entered his account and payment information.

Grin firmly in place, he double checked all the figures, then clicked CONFIRM, and waited. She'd get the notification right away. Any minute now, his phone would ring with a pissed-off Lily on the other end, waiting to give him an earful.

Beau checked his phone. Any minute now.

Two hours later, there was still no response and he started to get a little nervous. Surely, she must have seen it by now.

By noon the next day, he began to lose hope. Had he miscalculated? Was it possible she'd simply accepted the payment and moved on?

Stuck at home for the day because Marcus had barred him from the office until the trial, Beau checked his email inbox every ten minutes on the dot.

No new messages.

When six in the evening rolled by, Beau was forced to concede defeat. Lily was gone, and if his countermove hadn't stirred up enough feeling to get her to reach out, nothing would. She really didn't want him.

Collapsing on his bed, Beau gave in to the exhaustion that had been weighing on him ever since he'd left Miss Kiki's a week ago. With his head swimming and the whole world rocking around him like a massive boat on an angry sea, he closed his eyes and willed himself not to dream.

Just another bleak, lonely night. He'd now have a lifetime of them to look forward to.

"Next!"

As the side service door closed, the front door opened and Lily heard footsteps approaching.

Shifting into a more comfortable position on the settee, she said, as she had dozens of times over the last few days, "Shirt and shoes off. Put your resume here on the side table, and show me what you've got."

The rustle of fabric indicated the man either hadn't read those same instructions out in the waiting hall or he'd chosen to ignore them. Lily bit the inside of her cheek to keep from snapping at him. *Point deduction.*

Bare feet padded across the exquisite, lacquered floor toward her in a rhythm she'd learned to associate with an arrogant swagger. Then she felt the air displace against her bare skin as he came close, leaning over her. The settee shifted; he'd braced one hand on the edge for leverage. *Point deduction.*

"Proceed," she invited and almost immediately felt his breath against her neck and his hand at her breast. A lazy man's introduction. *Point deduction.* Nevertheless, what he was doing to her wasn't unpleasant. His lips were firm, his kisses just right, not too slobbery or too chaste. He touched her boldly—a man who knew what he liked and wasn't afraid to demand it. Confidence was a plus, but he seemed to be stuck on her breasts.

Lily braced her heel and cocked her hips up. He took the hint and his free hand left her breast and dove straight between her legs, completely ignoring the rest of her body. *Point deduction.* The guy might have good technique, but it was so limited, Lily felt bored.

Was he even worth this effort? She reached out to trace his body. Strong shoulders, good muscle definition in the arms, decent pecs and a tight stomach, and... "You're not hard."

The man raised his head from sucking her breast and asked, "Should I be?"

Lily pushed him back enough to allow her to sit up. She tore off her blindfold and glared at the thirty-something who seemed to think this was a joke. "Considering you're auditioning for the position of a *sex* worker, it might help to have the ability to get it up when called on."

His cheeks flushed angrily. "There are other ways to pleasure someone."

Lily rolled her eyes. Male number seventeen who'd tried to educate her about the pleasures of sex. *Instant disqualification.* "Take your stuff and go."

He seemed confused by that direction. "Excuse me?"

"Your audition is over. You failed. We will not be calling you back." To demonstrate how serious she was, she took his resume from the side table and dipped it into the shredder underneath. "Now go." Dismissing him from her mind, she yelled to the main door, "*Next!*"

The current candidate stared at her for a second longer, then scoffed and stormed back to his clothes. "Waste of fucking time."

Yes, you really were.

Three days into auditions, and Lily only had half of her roster filled. This should have been done and over in twenty-four hours. She couldn't afford any delays, especially now that she'd basically emptied her account to buy this place.

She'd had a massive stroke of celestial luck finding it right after her eviction. A recently vacated mansion in the noble district, with twenty-seven fully furnished rooms, thirty bathrooms, a servants' wing, and enough gild and frippery that Lily could open for business today. It had cost her a fortune, but it'd be worth it for the time and money she wouldn't have to spend renovating, furnishing, and cleaning.

But that didn't change the fact that she was now a destitute owner of a humongous house, with no manpower to fill it. She hadn't expected all her friends from Miss Kiki's to follow her, but she'd hoped that at least a few more would answer her invitation. In the end, Kendra had come knocking on her hotel door first thing the morning after the masquerade, with Peter and Michael in tow. Lacie and Pru had answered her email about coming over for a higher commission split, and Harley had said she'd consider it, but aside from that, most of the replies had been kind farewells and good luck wishes.

Not exactly comforting.

Lily couldn't run a twenty-seven room brothel with five workers. That would spell doom before she even opened the doors. And the longer these auditions stretched, the more uncomfortable her situation became. The others still had their own savings to tide them over for a while, but Lily was looking at one meal a day until they got up and running. She refused to take charity, and didn't want partners to dilute whatever profits her venture might bring—she'd need every last ducat to survive the initial stages.

To make her funds stretch longer, she'd been forced to sell off a painting or two from the mansion's luxurious decor. Pre-Zorana era family portraits didn't fetch much on today's markets, but the frames were antiques, and Lily had managed to haggle the price up enough that she could now afford to eat for a whole week, *and* pay the utilities bills at the end of the month.

But there was only so much stuff she could sell off, and with Auntie Dearest stiffing her of her final commission check, Lily had been forced to do the one thing she'd told herself she wouldn't.

The main door opened just as the previous candidate slammed the side entrance after him, bringing Lily back to her present frustration. Making an effort to focus on the task at hand, she shook herself out, tossed the blindfold aside, and turned a smile on the new applicant.

And immediately frowned.

The barefooted boy wringing his shirt in his hands looked absolutely terrified, padding forward as if he was walking up to the gallows. His hair might have been blond at one time, but now it was matted and dirty. Big, owl-like eyes stared at her out of a dirt-smudged face. He was skin and bones, clearly a street urchin who hadn't seen the business end of a bath in a very long time.

Just the sight of him made Lily's chest clench tight, and she wished she'd at least brought a blanket to cover her nakedness. But then, she'd never expected a *child* to walk through those doors.

"Who are you?" she asked, her voice sharper than she'd intended.

"M-my name is Matthew, ma'am. I-I'm here for the job."

Lily crooked her finger for him to come closer. "How old are you?"

"Eighteen, ma'am."

If he was a day over fifteen, Lily would eat his ratty shirt.

Gods, how desperate he had to be to come here.

"I was a street rat for as long as I can remember."

At the memory of Beau's nonchalant admission, Lily almost flinched. He'd said it as if it didn't matter whatsoever, as if it'd been a fun adventure for him to spend his childhood fighting to survive just one more day. She remembered listening to him talk about it like last week's news and aching for the little boy he'd been, wishing she could have helped him somehow.

Looking at Matthew now, Lily could easily imagine Beau in his place.

"Ma'am?"

Hope. That's what made it so awful to look at him. As desperate as he was, Matthew still had hope in his eyes that this crazy idea would work out for him. He was willing to offer his body to be used just so he could sleep under a solid roof.

Lily cleared her throat to find her voice. "Valefort has rules about this sort of thing, kid. Can't hire you as a sex worker until you reach the legal age of consent."

His narrow shoulders slumped and his chin quivered, but he rallied enough defiance to say, "I'm old enough!" It broke her heart.

"Not for this." When he looked as if he would start crying, she added, "But, I do have need of a kitchen boy." She totally didn't need a kitchen boy. Didn't even have a cook yet, or food for them to prepare. "You'd start with the menial tasks: washing dishes, taking out the trash, cleaning vegetables, running errands."

That hope in his brown eyes redoubled, making them look even bigger. "What's it pay?"

"Room and board to start right away. That means you'll live here and get three squares a day for your work. Once we open for business, fifteen ducats a day until the cook trusts you enough with more complicated tasks. Then we'll renegotiate."

He frowned in thought, stalling, even though Lily could see him all but quivering in anticipation. The boy had a mercenary side. She liked it. "Awright, I'll take it."

"Think it over," she cautioned. "This isn't a hotel. If looking at me naked makes you uncomfortable, you might want to consider going elsewhere. Here, you'll see far worse on a daily basis."

Matthew gave her a disinterested once-over and shrugged. "Seen worse already. Some of it's sitting out in the waiting room."

Lily snorted with a suppressed chuckle, teasing a shy smile out of the boy. He had strong, white teeth, at least. That was something. But the rest of him looked and smelled like he'd been living in the sewer.

"One more thing before we shake on it. You'll be enrolling in school and keeping your grades up at all times."

Matthew gaped. "But when will I have time to work?"

"I'll grant you one hour before school each day during the week, and two after. And all your homework will need to be finished and okayed by the cook before you start."

He made a face as if he'd rather scrub toilets all day than go to school. "And weekends?"

Man, he was persnickety. "Yours to do with as you please. If you want to work, clock in and have at it. If not, your choice."

Another thoughtful pause. "Suppose I'll have to clean up to work in a kitchen."

"Can't have dirt and lice in the stew," she agreed.

"I don't have lice!" he said, scratching hard at the back of his head.

Lily shrugged. "Do we have a deal?"

When she held out her hand, he looked at it, then met her gaze almost suspiciously. "Dunno what it is about you, lady, but I trust you. I'm in." He slapped his hand to hers and shook it vigorously.

"That's good to hear. Now go through that door, take a left, and go all the way to the back. There are some old uniforms in the laundry room, and soap in the bathroom right next to it. Next time I see you, you'd better be spotless. Got it?"

"Yes, ma'am!" He ran off so fast, it left her head spinning.

Adopting a kid into a brothel? Why the hell not?

Lily rubbed her forehead and picked up the walkie-talkie. "How many still in the waiting room?"

"Nine left," Kendra replied. "Then we have fifteen women coming in the afternoon."

"Can you take over for me? I need a break." Ten in the morning, and Lily felt as if she'd been up since midnight. Oh, wait, she *had* been.

"Not a problem. I'll take the guys. Peter and Michael can split the girls. We could have done the same with all of them, you know."

Yeah, they could have, but that would have left Lily with too much free time to think about things she didn't have time to think about.

Like how that achy hollow in her chest wasn't getting any smaller, or less achy. "Well, now's your chance. Make me proud, children." With that, she snuck out through the back door and dragged her feet up to her suite.

Maybe a nap would make her feel better.

No, there was still too much work to do. Dressing in her softest, worn jeans, she eschewed a bra in favor of a clingy tank top and oversized sweater, then fired up her computer. The new hires would begin moving in tomorrow, and she still didn't have a kitchen staff or a cleaning service lined up.

Luckily, she'd played this smarter than her aunt had. Her new employees might be getting a much higher commission, but in exchange they had to pay rent for the rooms and services they used, which meant that Lily would have a steady source of income, and very few expenses until business took off.

The question now was: Had the deposits cleared the bank yet? And would they be enough to start hiring staff?

Another perk of this place: built-in high-speed connection. Her bank website popped up in half a second. She typed in her credentials and logged on, bracing herself for the bleak picture about to load on the screen.

When it did, she did a double-take.

What?

No, that couldn't be right… Someone must have made a clerical error. She distinctly remembered there being two hundred and fifteen ducats in her account three days ago. With fifteen rent deposits rolling in, there should have been roughly three thousand ducats, give or take, depending on when they'd wired the funds. Where the hell had five hundred and sixty seven *thousand* ducats come from?

Lily looked over her shoulder, expecting to see Kendra or Peter standing there to yell, "Gotcha!" because this had to be a joke of some sort. A sick, cruel joke, but a joke nonetheless.

She clicked to expand the transaction history and found a six-figure deposit from two days ago, marked as "Payment: Invoice #12345."

Beau's invoice. The one she'd told herself she'd never write, and then had to write anyway, because she'd messed up setting up her business account and the bank had put a hold on the first rent deposits. She'd hated doing it, had charged him just enough to get her through a week or two out of necessity, and it sure as hell hadn't been a six-figure sum.

Had he screwed up the decimal points during payment?

Lily expanded the transaction and opened the attached receipt. Nope. He sure hadn't. He'd just decided to tack on a "tip" that was one hundred times the original invoice total. Was this supposed to be some kind of consolation prize? Damages to make up for her getting kicked out of Miss Kiki's? "Son of a bitch!"

Lily just prevented herself from throwing her computer. This would not be tolerated! Didn't matter how much easier that money would make everything, Lily refused to accept pity money from anyone, least of all *him*.

Stabbing her feet into a pair of sneakers, Lily snatched up her keys and phone on the way out the door.

Beau thought this would fix what he'd broken? He had a hell of a lot to learn about women.

Lily's school of Don't Fuck With A Redhead was about to go into session.

CHAPTER 18

Beau reached over to pick up the phone that wouldn't stop ringing. "H'llo."

"Beau! Where are you? Chang's trial starts in half an hour!"

Beau bolted upright. "What? Why didn't you call me sooner?"

"I've been ringing you all morning. What's wrong with you?"

He checked the clock. Ten thirty. *Shit!* "I'll be there in twenty minutes." Less, if he didn't change and ran the entire way. But he couldn't go to court looking like this. "Twenty-five at most. Stall if you can."

"Beau—"

He hung up and tossed the phone onto the bed. After the fastest cold shower of his life, he dug out his court garb: black pants, a simple white shirt and tie, and the traditional pleated black robe. And then he ran. Three blocks down, traffic was at a standstill, as it usually was when important business went on in the castle. He zigzagged between the cars and carriages, vaulted over the living fence, and cut across the royal gardens to the main gate.

Inside the courtyard, a mob of reporters crowded around the front door, the castle guard trying and failing to keep the exit clear. The prison coach was already parked off to the side, which meant Chang and his team of lawyers were already inside.

The tower bells began tolling the hour. Chang's trial had already begun and Beau still had to reach the courtroom in the bowels of the castle. Five minutes at a brisk walk. He could cut that down to two, running full tilt—

"Don't give me that shit, I know he's there somewhere! Get him out here—*now!*"

Lily?

Beau automatically turned the next right toward her voice instead of left for the courtroom. At the end of the hallway, Haig and Marcus, both dressed in their courtroom best, were facing off with one royally pissed-off redhead and looking seconds away from conceding defeat and running for the hills.

"Miss," Marcus said in his most kingly don't-fuck-with-me voice, "I already told you Beau's not available. You'll have to come back later."

"Or you can come with us to the trial," Haig offered. "He might be able to meet with you afterwards."

Might be able to? What the hell, Haig!

"Not good enough," Lily growled. "You call that rat bastard and tell him to get his ass over here right this freaking minute, or I swear—"

"Woman, your timing *sucks*," he called before she got herself tossed into a jail cell. Marcus did not tolerate threats from anyone.

Lily blinked at him, seeming momentarily at a loss for words. He didn't expect that to last very long.

"Beau," Haig warned, "you need to go to court. And I mean *right now.*"

"Darius will stall."

Haig gaped at him, and even Marcus raised an eyebrow. Neither of them had ever seen Beau even consider shirking his duties. They didn't understand how important this was.

"Can you give us a minute?"

Sharing a speaking look between them, the king and the rebel moved a few feet down the hallway. When he scowled at them, they moved a few more, not even bothering to pretend they weren't listening. Best he was going to get under the circumstances.

"Why are you dressed like that?" Lily demanded.

"I've got court," he said, hastily doing up the hook closures on his robes. "Chang's trial started a minute ago. I'm supposed to be giving the prosecution's opening statement. What are you doing here?"

"Five hundred and sixty *thousand* as a *tip*?" Her angry flush clashed with her hair and Beau wanted so badly to kiss it out of her.

Remember the plan. Yeah, the plan he'd budgeted two hours for, that he now had to execute in ninety seconds. Beau shrugged. "Tips are at the customer's discretion, as I understand it."

Lily sputtered. "Half a million ducats is not a *tip*, asshole, it's a charitable donation. Do I look like a charity to you?"

Variation 12-B, condensed by a factor of ten. "No, you look like someone who just lost her only source of income and should probably be grateful for any extra money coming her way."

Behind him, Haig and Marcus groaned.

Lily gasped. "The nerve… Astounding!"

"You're looking at this all wrong."

Haig hissed, muttering something about "Bad play."

"Oh, I can't wait to hear this," Lily said, crossing her arms over her chest. Her foot tapped out an angry rhythm.

Beau had expected this, but didn't have the time to play out the full round of his argument. Sixty seconds. "Don't think of it as money from *me*. It's more of a reward for helping to capture a traitor—"

"Okay, I can't take this anymore." Marcus stepped between them, motioning to the other rebel. "Haig, why don't you take Ms. Maverick to the waiting room. I need to have a word with Beau."

"Better talk some sense into him before I make his face a lot less pretty," Lily grated as Haig bodily pulled her away.

Marcus dragged Beau to the next door over, giving him a shove across the threshold. "Boy, you are embarrassing me. What the hell is wrong with you?"

"I don't have time for this!"

"I've seen you talk down suicide bombers with more grace than you just showed out there! Don't tell me you can't handle one little redhead."

"Oh, you mean the redhead even you were about to run from?"

Marcus rolled his shoulders. "I am the king. I must survive to beget heirs."

Beau rolled his eyes.

Marcus looked around for something, then seemed to make a decision and sat on the edge of a desk. "If you can't talk to her, you'd better talk to me. I assume you still have some kind of feelings for this woman?"

If he wasn't so freaked out, Beau would have laughed at that. Hysterically. But Marcus had his serious face on, which meant, trial or no trial, they were not leaving until this got resolved. Beau hung his head and sat in one of the plush armchairs.

"I must apologize for Beau," Haig said with his signature player smile. Every time he flashed it at Miss Kiki's, girls dropped trou and proffered panties. Lily didn't see the appeal. "He's not usually so…"

"Coarse? High-handed? Insulting?"

"Tactless," Haig said, his smile dimming. "In fact, now that I think about it, I've never seen him bungle something this badly. Whatever happened between you two, it must have twisted him up pretty bad."

Lily snorted. "I seriously doubt that."

Haig raised an eyebrow. He sat behind the desk and waved her on.

Ignoring the empty seat across from him, Lily paced to the window and back to the door. "It doesn't matter, anyway. He's the queen's right hand man and I'm just a lowly whore. Better for everyone if we go our separate ways."

"Did he tell you that?"

"He didn't have to."

"I think you're misreading the situation—"

"Great! Another man trying to tell me what to think."

"I just meant—"

The desk phone beeped, and then the king's voice came through the intercom speaker. "If you can't talk to her, you'd better talk to me. I assume you still have some kind of feelings for this woman?"

Frowning, Haig held a finger to his lips for silence, then reached over to mute the microphone. Then he waved her closer.

"What is this?"

Haig cocked his head. "If I had to guess, I'd say it's a singular chance for you to peek into the inner workings of Beau's mind. If you want to."

Did she?

"Come on, Beau," the king said. "It's a simple question. Do you still care about her?"

"*Care?*" Beau repeated. "I *care* about Snow. But Lily…" His pause was so long she almost passed out from holding her breath. "I don't even know how to describe it. She's like a drug that's made me sick with withdrawals for ten years and now I got another dose. I think this one was lethal, Marcus."

Lily's knees gave out and she sat down on the edge of the desk, hanging on every rustle of sound coming from that speaker, aware that Haig was studying her every reaction.

"The word you're looking for," the king of Valefort said carefully, "is love. You're lovesick for the girl who stole your heart before you even knew what was what."

"Is it always this painful?"

She gasped. He hadn't denied it!

"Not if she loves you back."

A sigh. "She doesn't." *What?!* "I thought she might have started to care for me, but I was wrong. You should have seen her that night. She couldn't get away from me fast enough."

That's why he hadn't called all this time? He thought *she'd* left *him*?

"Wouldn't even look at me."

Lily pressed a hand to her mouth. No, she hadn't really looked at him. She'd been too hurt by his casual tone, too angry with the situation, and too desperate to get out of there to realize there might have been more behind his words.

My man's a doer, not a talker.

Gods, he'd asked her to move in with him! Not out of obligation, but because he'd wanted her.

"Did you *tell* her you love her?"

"No," Beau admitted.

"Really, Beau?"

Yeah, really, Beau?

"You don't understand! Everything went wrong with Chang—and I mean *everything*—and she got caught in the crossfire. What was I supposed to say after that? What *could* I have possibly said that wouldn't have come across like a slap in the face? 'Sorry you lost your home and a job you loved, but I'm here for you so you don't have to work in a brothel anymore'?"

She would have ripped him to shreds if he'd tried that tack.

"I did what I could, offered for her to move in with me, you know, no pressure, ball's in your court kind of deal." He scoffed. "Boy, did that *not* work at all."

"So your countermeasure was to wait a week and then pay her a six-figure tip? That seemed like a smart idea?"

She could almost hear the helpless shrug in Beau's voice when he replied, "I didn't want to crowd her. She's independent to a fault. And she never hinted that she might feel something for me." *Letting you live with me for two weeks wasn't enough of a hint?* "Actually, she went out of her way to tell me she *didn't* need me."

Lily winced at that, instantly regretting everything she'd said to him that night. How could she have misjudged him this much?

"I thought… I *hoped* that once she calmed down she might miss me and reach out. When all I got was the invoice, I thought that was it, you know? Her brand of closure. And I figured if I did this, at least I'd get to see her one more time…"

Lily was out the door before he'd finished speaking. She yanked open the other office door to hear him finish in person, "…planned to have more than ninety seconds to explain—"

"You're an idiot, you know that?"

Beau looked from her to the king.

King Marcus shrugged, standing from the desk. "Oops," he said without apology. "Must have sat on the intercom button. Clumsy me. Come on, Haig, we've got a traitor to sentence. Beau, you have five minutes, then I expect you in that courtroom. Understood?"

Without waiting for an answer, he went out the door, dragging a sputtering Haig in his wake. "Hey, I was watching that!" The door closed behind them.

Beau pushed to his feet. "Lily, I—"

"Shut up." She threw herself at him, arms clutching around his neck, legs around his waist, and stamped her mouth on his to stop him from saying anything more stupid. He stumbled back on impact, but managed to right himself, and then his arms were around her, and he was kissing her back, and *finally* that hollow ache in her chest began to ease, pieces of her broken heart melting back together to make a solid whole.

Gods, she'd missed this so much!

Too soon, he broke away. "I love you, Lily."

Her heart soared. "You have no idea how long I've waited to hear you say that," she said, so giddy she could hardly contain it.

"Two weeks?"

"Uh-uh, lover boy. Try ten years."

He frowned, then his eyes went wide as he finally put two and two together.

Lily pressed a soft kiss to his lips. "Why did you think I gambled for that kiss?" Another kiss to his jaw. "Beau Legeare, I have loved you since the day you stole the last jam pastry from the supply loot for me our first day in the mine."

Beau nuzzled her temple. "I remember that. You were just this scrawny little thing, looked absolutely terrified."

"I was. Until you."

He sighed. "I have to go to court." Yet instead of letting her go, he clutched her even tighter.

"Yes," Lily agreed. The last thing she wanted to do was let him walk out that door, but after everything they'd been through to get this far, Chang had better not walk on a technicality like Beau's absence. So she unhooked her ankles and leaned back until he set her on her feet. "Go on. Go save the day like you always do. I'll be here waiting for you when you're ready."

"I promise I won't make you wait too long."

"Dearest love, who says I'd let you?"

About the Author

ALIANNE DONNELLY was a wordsmith long before she became a reader. Driven by an insatiable curiosity about everything from history and mythology to science and philosophy, she grew into a fiction writer who hates coloring inside the genre lines. Her books all have elements of romance, with different series sorted under paranormal, science fiction, fantasy, and erotic. And then there's *Wolfen*…

Alianne lives in California, doing hard time in a corporate 9-5, while secretly scribbling away any chance she gets. She loves pizza, hiking, and avoiding small talk, and hopes to one day win the lottery jackpot.

9 781948 325332